Kerry decided not to wait for Nemesis to catch up with her, but to take the initiative. She would apologise, but she would not eat humble pie. She might have treated the town's leading surgeon as though he were a medical student, but she had done it out of concern for his son. Her voice was firm and confident as she said, 'I owe you an apology, Dr Travis.'

'Oh?' he said absentmindedly. Though his eyes were on her face, she knew he had not heard a word she had said. Clearly, Alicia still occupied his mind to the exclusion of everything else, thought Kerry, exasperated, yet at the same time relieved that there seemed no point in pursuing the conversation further.

She moved slightly, intending to pick up her handbag which was lying on the corner of the coffee table. Before she could do so, his arms, as hard as steel, were around her, and his mouth was on hers, forcing her head back.

She was so completely taken by surprise that for several stunned moments she could not move, could not think. Just one word drummed in her mind. Alicia. Alicia. . .

For Judith Hunte, writing Doctor Nurse romances is a happy merging of two major interests, nursing and writing. Judith worked for several years as a librarian before beginning nursing training, eventually qualifying as a registered nurse and midwife. She left nursing to marry and have her family, a son and two daughters, then returned to work in various Australian hospitals for several years.

Early retirement has given her the opportunity to indulge a lifelong yen to write. Her own nursing experience provides the background for her stories.

THE HEALING OF DR TRAVIS

BY

JUDITH HUNTE

MILLS & BOON LIMITED
ETON HOUSE 18-24 PARADISE ROAD
RICHMOND SURREY TW9 1SR

First published in Great Britain 1988
by Mills & Boon Limited

This edition 1988

ISBN 0 263 76175 4

Set in Baskerville 10 on 11 pt.
03 – 8809 – 56835

Typeset in Great Britain by JCL Graphics, Bristol

Made and printed in Great Britain

CHAPTER ONE

'WELL? What do you think?'

Kerry Martyn turned from the mirror after putting a last clip in the diminutive piece of starched muslin perched on her honey-blonde hair, and looked, somewhat anxiously, at Jo Stephenson, who was sitting carefully on the edge of Kerry's bed so as not to crease her crisp white starched uniform.

Jo marvelled that the other girl, the newest addition to the staff of the Mount Myall District and Community Hospital, seemed less than satisfied with her appearance. Jo, whose curly brown hair, warm blue eyes and wide smile added up to a pleasing attractiveness rather than beauty, could see nothing amiss with Kerry's delicately moulded features, her flawless complexion, her lovely blue-grey eyes. She answered Kerry's question with the only word that seemed appropriate.

'Perfect!'

'But how old do I look?'

'About eighteen.'

Kerry made a moue of disgust.

'That's what I was afraid of. I hoped that putting my hair up would help, but apparently it hasn't.'

'So that's the reason for the French roll. But why try to look old before your time? I think eighteen is a lovely age.'

'I do, too—for a new pro! But I'm twenty-three, fully trained and about to start my first job as an RN, for which Matron seems to think I'm too young.'

'Did she say that?' asked Jo.

'Not in as many words. But she looked so amazed when she saw me for the first time, last evening. At first I thought it was because of how I was dressed. She's asked to see me as soon as I arrived, because she was about to go off duty, so I had no option but to front up for my first interview with her dressed in blue demin shorts up to here'—indicated the top of her thigh—'bare legs and an old pair of sneakers. I didn't even have time to comb my hair.'

'Matron would have realised you'd been travelling all day,' said Jo.

'Yes. She really didn't seem too fazed by my gear. That was why I decided it must be my age that bothered her.'

Jo eyed Kerry's tiny waist and trim figure with something like envy. 'Perhaps it wasn't your age as much as the fact that you do look somewhat . . . fragile. Matron is more used to buxom country lasses than Dresden figurines. Incidentally, that was quite an accomplishment, driving all the way from Sydney on your own.'

Kerry laughed. 'You'll be even more impressed when you've seen my car! It's a beat-up little bomb I bought from a medical student in a weak moment because he needed the money. My brother thought I was crazy to attempt six hundred kilometres in it. He probably sat by the phone all day, waiting for a rescue call.'

'And you had no problems?'

'No mechanical problems. There was an incident late in the day, but it was more intriguing than problematical.'

Kerry was thoughtful. Perhaps Jo could throw some light on that incident. But she could hear footsteps hurrying past her door and Jo was standing up, smoothing down her uniform. Time for work. Kerry reached for her red cape which was lying on the bed and drew a deep breath.

Jo smiled at her. 'Butterflies?' she asked sympathetically.

'Some,' Kerry admitted. 'In fact I *feel* like a new pro on my first day on the wards now. I'm glad you called in for me, Jo.'

'You'll do fine. Kids' Ward is more or less on my way to OR. I'll have time to detour and introduce you to Sister Dutton. And the p.m. shift shouldn't present too many problems.'

They arrived at the head of the staircase at the same moment as two other girls in white uniforms. Kerry had already met Vicki and was introduced to Sue Jamieson. They descended the stairs, crossed the foyer and passed through the wide front door of the Nurses' Home in a chattering group. They skirted a tennis court, then followed a path across a wide expanse of lawn to a back entrance of the hospital.

With one ear on the conversation of the other girls, Kerry was thinking back over the previous day, wondering how long it would be before there was a sequel to that episode on the road towards the end of her journey.

That incident, she admitted now, in the clearer light of the day after, had been trivial enough. It was her reaction to it that she found hard to understand, even allowing for the fatigue she had been feeling after driving so far.

She had left Sydney at eight that morning, laughing at her brother's cautionary admonitions and mutterings about medical students who, he hoped, would one day be better at looking after their patients than they were at maintaining their cars.

Her family could not understand her decision to go so far from Sydney to continue her nursing career. To them, Sydney was the hub of the universe, and everything one needed for a full and happy life could be found within its beautiful, frenetic, cosmopolitan confines.

Kerry loved Sydney too, and, as she approached the Bridge that morning from North Sydney and glimpsed the sparkling waters of the Harbour on her left, dotted, even at this hour, with skimming sails beneath blue, blue sky, she knew a moment of doubt about her decision to leave it. Mount Myall was south-west of Sydney, inland and far from the sea which she loved.

The doubt became a pang as she realised that, at that very moment, in a steep, wooded cove off Middle Harbour, Tony would be preparing the boat for a day on the water. She could have been there with him, as she had so many times before, pottering round the boat with him, bare brown limbs soaking up the sun, loving the feel of the wind on her face and in her hair.

She smiled to think of the almost convincing performance of a young man crossed in love that Tony had given when she had told him she was leaving Sydney. Apart from one early, brief sortie into romance, friendship had been the name of the game for them. But it had been a good friendship and she wondered whether absence would deepen their feelings for one another. She thought not. Tony's absorption in his boat was as complete as hers in her career. He would find someone else to crew for him and she would become absorbed into the life of her new hospital.

Exhilarated by the prospect and the challenges ahead of her, she caught the eye of an elderly gentleman in a car stopped beside hers at a traffic light, and smiled gaily at him. He returned the smile and went on his way when the light turned green, envying the chap who could bring a look like that to such a pretty face, and regretting his own long-lost youth.

Nine hours later, Kerry's exhilaration had been

replaced by a sense of satisfaction at having so nearly completed her journey, and by some slight nervous anticipation of her arrival.

The late afternoon sun was casting a dazzling kaleidoscope of light and shade across the road through tall gum trees that bordered it. Her eyes felt tired, her legs were stiff and her hair dishevelled from driving with the window open. She would look for a service station where she could stop and freshen up before driving the last twenty or so kilometres.

A few kilometres farther on she saw a tiny service station, nestled in the shade of a huge eucalypt. It seemed the ideal place to stop, and she pulled in beside the only petrol pump, as a gangling, red-haired youth in battered blue jeans ambled across the yard to serve her. He was slow of speech, slow of movement, and was still passing the time of day with Kerry when a sleek silver-grey Mercedes glided in off the road and stopped immediately behind Kerry's car.

She was amused by the incongruity of the large limousine nudging her Maxi's tiny bumper bar, and her face was lit by a smile as she caught the eye of the driver of the other car. But there was no glimmer of response on his face. Rather, he was staring at her with a curiously intent gaze while the fingers of his right hand drummed on the steering wheel in front of him. Clearly, he was impatient at the delay being caused him, and Kerry turned away to urge the lad operating the pump to hurry. Then, irresistibly compelled to do so, she looked back at the man. He was still studying her face, almost as though he was startled to see her. She was disconcerted and slightly embarrassed, but this time she refused to drop her eyes before his, and returned look for look.

Through the window of his car, Kerry had the impression that the man was slim and quite tall. He had strong, regular features beneath thick, wavy brown hair, and a lift to his head which bespoke a self-confidence bordering on arrogance. His eyes were dark brown, and Kerry wondered, suddenly, whether it was not, after all, impatience that she saw in them, but something deeper. Bitterness, perhaps? Tragedy, even?

As though he did not know or did not care that she was looking at him, his eyes moved now, very slowly and missed nothing, down to her feet, then back to her face again. She was acutely conscious of the slight breeze moulding the thin cotton of her blouse to the curve of her breasts, of her brief blue demin shorts, her long bare legs and the old pair of sneakers on her feet. She was used enough to admiring glances from men not to be unduly bothered by them. But there was no admiration in this man's scrutiny and, she thought, no sexual overtones either. Rather, it seemed coldly clinical, causing her to feel like something small and defenceless under a microscope.

Although embarrassed, she refused to be intimidated by him and, with a small, defiant toss of the head, said, 'I shan't be long.' She knew he could not hear her through the closed window of his no doubt air-conditioned car, but he must have caught her meaning. He gave no indication that he had done so but turned and spoke briefly to a woman in the passenger seat behind him. As the woman turned her head towards him, Kerry glimpsed a classically beautiful profile and a gleam of smooth blonde hair.

Whatever the man had said caused the woman to flick a disdainful glance at the small tableau in front of them—taking in the scrubby youth at the pump, the ancient little car, the girl with dishevelled honey-blonde hair curling about her shoulders and large, red-rimmed sunglasses pushed on top of her head. Kerry knew that she looked as much in keeping with that down-at-heel little scenario the couple were surveying, as they did in their glossy Mercedes.

Without her in the least understanding why, the man in the Mercedes intrigued her, embarrassed though she was by his scrutiny of herself. But the woman was blatantly supercilious, and suddenly Kerry was angry. She did not have to suffer this situation a moment longer. Thrusting a ten-dollar note at the attendant who had, at long last, completed his task, and saying, 'Keep the change,' she walked around to the driver's seat of her car with her head held high and got behind the wheel. Jabbing one foot at the clutch pedal and the other at the accelerator, she shot out on to the road, the Maxi's tyres squealing a protest and slithering wildly as they hit the smooth bitumen.

Even as Kerry fought to bring the car under control, she was aware of the couple in the Mercedes, still watching her, and she gritted her teeth in chagrin. She could imagine what the woman was thinking, but this did not bother her. The man was clearly a male chauvinist pig and, after witnessing her appalling display of incompetent driving, would be more than ever convinced that a woman should not be allowed behind the wheel of a car.

So what! she told herself. She would never see either of them again. She must stop thinking about them and pull her shattered composure together so that she could arrive at the hospital with some degree of equanimity.

She wondered whether she should stop by the side of the road and comb her hair and repair her make-up as she had not had a chance to do at the service station, but decided to press on and hope to be in time for a shower before the hospital evening meal.

After a time, the road began to twist and turn into a range of low hills, thickly wooded right down to the roadside. A sign warned, 'Winding Road—7k.' and beneath it, an advisory speed sign—'35k.' The road had a single lane in either direction and, knowing that the Maxi did not perform well on hills, Kerry glanced in her rear vision mirror, hoping she would not soon have a trail of cars behind her. Her hope was ill-founded. A car was already sliding into view around the last curve and, with a sinking heart, she realised that it was the grey Mercedes.

She should have known it would overtake her, since it had been travelling in the same direction as she. But why did it have to be here, where it was quite impossible to pass her? The driver of the Mercedes had clearly not accepted the impossibility of passing. He had rapidly closed the gap between them and slowed down behind her, much too close for comfort, looking for an opportunity to speed by.

He was certainly in a hurry to get somewhere. But the double yellow line in the centre of the road was uncompromising and there was no grassy verge or convenient lay-by where she could pull over and let him through. In her mirror Kerry glimpsed a frown of exasperation on the dark, handsome face. All she could do was raise one hand in a gesture which said, Sorry—nothing I can do! Then she gave all her attention to guiding the Maxi round the sometimes hazardous curves as quickly as possible, thinking that she could perhaps, at the same time, retrieve her reputation as a good driver.

Finally, after minutes that seemed like hours, they reached the top of the range, the road widened out, Kerry pulled to the left as far as she could and slowed down with a sigh of relief. The car behind accelerated and sped past. Happy to see the last of it and its occupants, she waved cheerfully as it went by. The man raised one hand in brief, unsmiling acknowledgement. The woman looked straight ahead.

Ships that pass in the night, thought Kerry, and turned

her attention to the scene below her, as she slowly followed the road that wound on down into the valley.

It was a beautiful valley. A double line of trees marked the course of a small river through it. Lush green pastures were broken here and there by a brown, ploughed paddock or clump of trees. Prosperous-looking homesteads were enclosed by white fences or rows of tall populars or gum trees. At the far end of the valley, at the foot of an opposing line of hills, sprawled a large town which must be Mount Myall. And somewhere there was the hospital which was to be Kerry's home for the foreseeable future. With quickening heartbeat, she accelerated, down on into the valley.

In the town she stopped to ask the way to the hospital of a tired schoolboy on a bicycle with a pair of football boots slung by its laces round his neck. The hospital was on the far side of town, the last building before the hills and bushland took over again. It was a modern building of warm cream brick, rising four storeys at its centre with wide double-storeyed wings on either side. The backdrop of hills provided a perfect foil for landscaped gardens, bright with summer annuals, in front of the hospital.

Kerry turned slowly into the broad driveway across the front of the building. She had been instructed to report to Reception on arrival. A parking area near the entrance was For Doctors Only. She was about to drive on when she saw, with a jolt of stunned disbelief, the silver-grey Mercedes, standing in the doctors' car park, as if very sure of its place in the hierarchy of the Mount Myall Hospital.

Kerry by now had an automatic reaction of dismay at the sight of the Mercedes, but this was followed quickly by the realisation that the Mercedes man must be a doctor. And a senior one, at that, by the look of things. The implications of this discovery dawned on her. A doctor hurrying to a hospital on a Saturday afternoon would most likely have been called to an emergency. In that case, any delay would have been frustrating to him. No wonder he had seemed impatient!

With quick empathy for anything to do with her profession, Kerry forgave him, fully and freely, for what she had deemed to be rudeness on his part. His mind could well have been preoccupied with the problem of his patient. He possibly had been, in fact, looking at her without seeing her at all. She smiled to think how she had allowed her imagination to run riot, seeing things like tragedy and bitterness in his face.

As she parked the Maxi in an area farther on and walked back towards the entrance, she was thinking, with a tingle of expectation, that she was bound to meet the Mercedes doctor sooner or later, in the course of their duties. Would he recognise her? Would she ever know him well enough to discuss the encounter at the service station with him, perhaps laugh about it together?

Passing the Mercedes again, she registered that the passenger seat was empty also. She had assumed earlier that the woman in the car with him was his wife or his girlfriend. But wives or girlfriends did not usually accompany their partners on hospital calls. The woman could be a member of the staff—the Matron, even?

As Kerry passed through self-opening doors into a cool, blue-carpeted foyer, she was devoutly hoping that that would not be so, and was immensely relieved, a few minutes later, to be ushered into the presence of a very traditional Matron in a long-sleeved white uniform and wide white veil—the antithesis of the lady in the car.

After the interview, Kerry had been caught up into the world within the hospital, meeting new people, having tea in the staff dining room, unpacking. She had dropped, early and wearily, into bed and slept soundly.

Indeed, she had not thought again about the couple in the Mercedes until her conversation with Jo this morning had reminded her of it.

CHAPTER TWO

'BE SEEING YOU, Jo! Have a good day, Kerry!'

They had reached the hospital building and, inside, Sue and Vicki's paths diverged. They went off to Women's Medical in the East Wing, leaving Jo and Kerry to take an elevator to the third floor. Here, in a noisy, cheerful highly colourful Children's Wing, Jo introduced Kerry to Sister Dutton who was tiny and grey-haired, with alert black eyes and a brisk manner.

'Please to have you, Sister. Sit yourself down while I write a few obs into my report.'

Kerry added her cape to the collection of red and blue ones already hanging behind the door of the duty room, and seated herself at the other end of Sister's table.

She felt reassured at once by the familiarity of it all—the sphygmomanometer on the table, the trolley of case notes, lists of medications and treatments, encased in plastic, a large pin-up board with notices of meetings and social functions, humorous clippings and a couple of clever pen drawings.

A slim, blonde, pretty girl with threee stripes on her cap drifted in, smiled shyly at Kerry and stood waiting. Sister looked at her watch and said, 'Now! If Nurse Baker will favour us with her presence . . .' As if on cue, Nurse Baker erupted into the room, bringing a whiff of cigarette smoke and putting a last pin in a cap which perched precariously on a mountain of teased auburn hair. She stopped abruptly, blurted, 'Sorry Sister!' and looked with curiosity at Kerry.

Sister introduced the two nurses to Kerry, cast a

quelling glance at Nurse Baker who was still adjusting her cap, and began to read her report. Nurse Baker dropped her hands, clasped them behind her back and riveted her attention on the report. Kerry, so lately a nurse herself, suspected that Baker was more interested in planning the where and how of her next cigarette than in what Sister was saying. Then Kerry turned her own attention to the report, making mental notes of several salient points while planning to follow her usual practice in a new ward where she did not know her patients. She would re-read the report as soon as Sister had left, in conjuction with the case notes of each patient, and then do a ward round and make the acquaintance of her small charges. By then, every detail of their diagnosis, history, treatment and prognosis would be firmly fixed in her mind.

When the report was finished, the two nurses departed. Sister said to Kerry, 'Nurse Snow is an excellent girl, quiet but responsible. Baker works reasonably well if you keep behind her. You should have a quiet afternoon. All the doctors have done rounds and the only one who might come back is Dr McManus, for Michelle, the myringotomy with the elevated temperature. Now, the drugs!'

She led the way out of the duty room and around a corner to a room, little more than a cupboard, which she unlocked, then unlocked another compartment inside. Side by side, she and Kerry counted the dangerous drugs, each ampoule, each tablet. They both signed the book, Sister locked everything again and handed the keys to Kerry, who pinned them to the inside of her pocket.

'Goodbye and good luck.' Sister walked, slowly now, as though she were suddenly tired, along the corridor and out of sight.

Kerry turned to go back to the duty room. A man in a dark grey suit was standing with his back to her, near the door of the duty room. She had no time to think that there was something vaguely familiar about him, before he turned at the sound of her footsteps.

It was the Mercedes man.

Momentarily, Kerry felt breathless with the surprise of the meeting, which, although it had to come some time, was the last thing she was expecting at the moment.

She had almost bumped into him as she turned the corner, and felt quite overpowered by his presence. He must be at least six feet two inches tall and the proud lift of his head made him seem even taller. Kerry automatically stepped back a pace—she could not hold a conversation with him at such close proximity, though she had not the slightest notion how to initiate such a conversation. Her mind was quite blank.

He too seemed at a loss to know what to say. There was the barest flicker of surprise and recognition in his dark eyes when they had first lighted on Kerry, but it had gone as quickly as it came and there was a blankness now on his handsome features, as though he were purposely suppressing whatever it was he was feeling.

He was the first to break the silence, by asking brusquely, 'Where's Sister?'

Kerry replied quietly, 'I'm in charge of Children's Ward this afternoon. May I help you?'

He looked at her as though finding it difficult to digest what she had said. Then, with a slight shake of his head, as though to remind himself of where he was and what his purpose was in being there, he replied, 'Yes, you may. I want to know when David last had medication.'

In spite of his distinguished appearance, his perfectly tailored suit, his aura of dignity and grooming, his manner was objectionable and overbearing. Without resorting to words, he managed to convey that he was a man who did not suffer fools gladly and that he considered her to be one.

She could not understand his attitude and she resented it. He had no way of knowing her capabilities as a nurse, yet already, she felt, he had weighed her in the balance and found her wanting. It was almost impossible to believe that he could still be upset about the delay she had caused him yesterday. Perhaps she should apologise? No, that would be to give the incident more significance than she felt it deserved.

He was waiting for her answer to his question. She tried to recall the report. It would be nice to be able to give him the information he sought, but of no great consequence if she could not. It was only a matter of consulting the child's case-notes to ascertain it. David? That would be David Travis, six years old, asthmatic, on aerosol Ventolin four-hourly SOS. So far, so good. But when had he last had it? She knew she had drawn a blank.

She said, 'I'm sorry, It don't know when David last had medication . . .' She was about to add that she would check his case-notes and made a move to step past him, but he interjected rudely.

'You mean to say that you're the Sister in charge of this ward, and yet you don't know a simple detail like that about one of the patients in your care?'

The sheer injustice of it left Kerry speechless. If he were one of the hospital's regular visiting doctors he must know that she was new to the hospital. He would also be familiar with ward routine and would know that she had been on duty less than half an hour. For some reason, he was not prepared to make allowances—had determined to see her in the worst possible light. If only he had come ten minutes later, she could have given him the information he sought. Or if he had come ten minutes earlier Sister Dutton would still have been there. They seemed to be fated to meet each other at the worst possible times, as they had on the road yesterday. Five minutes either way would have made all the difference there too.

She stood very straight and returned stare for hostile stare, unabashed, though she kept her tone of voice respectful.

'I'll get David's case-notes.' Moving towards the duty room, she added coolly, 'I assume you are his doctor?'

He said, sharply, 'I'm not his doctor. I happen to be his father.' And he followed her into the room.

Kerry was taken aback. She had seen his car in the doctors' parking lot yesterday. It seemed that she had jumped to the wrong conclusion. Perhaps he was a favoured VIP of the town who parked where he wished. Certainly he had enough effrontery to do so.

But, if he were not a doctor, it put a whole new complexion on their present situation. Fathers, even domineering, self-assertive fathers like this one, should not be in the duty room, and certainly should not be allowed to read their sons' case-notes, as this one had every intention of doing, standing with hand extended, to take the file from her. Kerry held on to it and stood her ground firmly.

'I'm sorry,' she said, neither sounding nor feeling it, 'parents are not permitted to see their children's case-notes. If you'll wait outside, I'll check on David's medication. Although, you know,' she continued, warming to her role of Sister in charge of the situation, 'you can safely leave the management of that to your son's doctor and to the nursing staff.'

There was a sardonic gleam in his eyes as he allowed her to finish her speech. Then suddenly, surprisingly, his mouth twitched into what could almost have been called a smile.

'Oh dear!' he said, with an exaggerated sigh. 'We do seem to have got ourselves into a contretemps! Since you're obviously new here, I suppose I should have introduced myself at the beginning of this unfortunate conversation.'

Kerry could not have agreed more, but she bit off the retort that rose to her lips and remained silent.

'I *am* David's father,' he continued. 'I am also a doctor—Dr Simon Travis. My partner is looking after David and, I assure you, has no objection to my seeing his medical notes.'

Kerry felt herself flush with embarrassment. Then she was angry. He was right—the simple courtesy of an introduction would have spared them this whole unpleasant scene. But his man, she decided, for all his air of superiority, did not seem to know the basic rules of courtesy.

And why his open show of hostility? He must be a very petty man if the reason for his conduct today really was resentment at the delay she had caused him yesterday.

He was waiting, looking at her with an expression she could not read. But obviously the ball was in her court.

'I'm Kerry Martyn,' she said curtly.

'I'm pleased to meet you . . . again . . . Sister Kerry Martyn,' he said mockingly.

So he *had* recognised her. Kerry had the unpleasant feeling that he was playing some sort of cat-and-mouse game with her. The trouble was she did not know the name of the game, nor the rules by which it was played. Until she had some idea of what it was all about she would have to go very circumspectly, saying very little, and, if possible, not reacting to the needling of her.

But now, without giving her a chance to say anything further, had she wished to do so, and as if he were impatient himself of whatever game he was playing, he said, 'Now could we please attend to David? He was quite dyspnoeic when I left him and will no doubt be worse by now.'

Kerry consulted the notes in her hand, gathering the shreds of her authority about her by not handing them to him, and said, 'It's just over three hours since he had a mask, but there's no need to wait the full four hours if he needs another. I'll attend to it.'

'Thank you, Sister.' His tone of voice was meek enough, but she knew he was mocking her again.

She held her head high and followed him into a ward with two cots and two beds. The cots were empty. In one bed a mother was quietly reading to a sleepy small girl. Dr Wilson's ventral hernia, thought Kerry, then turned to the bed beside which Dr Travis was standing.

The child in the bed was not unlike his father. He had the same regular features and the same brown eyes. But his hair was golden, and, where the father's expression was arrogant, the son's was soft and tentative, with the anxious look of the chronic asthmatic. He was a beautiful child. Yet it was not his beauty that instantly appealed to Kerry, but his vulnerability.

He was looking from his father to her, from beneath long lashes, and Kerry had the feeling, oddly, that it was not her presence but his father's which was making him nervous. She wished the man would sit down so he would not seem so overpowering, both to herself and to the child.

She sat down on the side of the bed so that her face was level with his and took his hand in hers so she could unobtrusively check his pulse rate. The sign over the bed said Davey, and she said, 'Hullo, Davey. I'm Sister Martyn. Daddy tells me it's time for another mask.'

She herself was not so sure the mask was necessary. Though his chest was heaving slightly, he was not unduly distressed and his colour was good, with no telltale cyanosis of lips or fingernails. She suspected that Dr Travis might have been over-anxious in asking for the medication, but she was not about to cross swords with him over that. And his concern for his son was the first positive and likeable thing she had found in the man.

She carefully measured the prescribed amount of Ventolin broncho-dilating solution, then added the sterile diluting fluid. 'Now,' she said to Davey, 'what do you want to be this time—an astronaut or a fire-fighter?'

'A fire-fighter,' said Davey shyly.

'Right-ho! Here comes Captain David Travis to the rescue.' Kerry popped the small plastic mask over Davey's face and adjusted the strap behind his head. Two wide brown eyes regarded her with interest, as he breathed in and out obediently, obviously well accustomed to the treatment. She suspected that her small makebelieve ploy had been unnecessary. Something else for Dr Travis to mock about, she thought.

Dr Travis had not spoken since entering the room. He no longer looked self-confident, seeming even to be a little ill at ease, as parents often are in the unfamiliar environment of a hospital. But this man was a doctor; he would be as much at home in a hospital ward as in his own sitting room. Kerry glancing at him, wondering, surprised, whether it was yearning that she saw in his eyes.

David seemed to accept his father's silence as though he were accustomed to it. He was watching the bed opposite, where Lindy's mother was reading to her daughter. Wishing to break the silence which was fast becoming uncomfortable, and remembering the passenger in Dr Travis's car yesterday, Kerry said cheerfully, as she removed the mask, 'I suppose your mother will be in to see you later on, Davey.'

Davey dropped his eyes and said nothing. Dr Travis's face and voice were devoid of expression as he said flatly, 'David doesn't have a mother.'

Kerry's discomfiture was complete. She wanted nothing, now, but to get out of the presence of this . . . this . . . overbearing, supercilious man who seemed to have the ability to put her in the wrong at every turn.

She refused to allow her embarrassment to show as she finished wiping Davey's face and stowing away the mask. She patted his shoulder and smiled, 'See you later, young man,' then turned to leave the room as quickly as she could, barely managing to control the trembling that had suddenly afflicted her legs.

Something made her look back as she reached the door. Dr Travis was watching her and there was a curiously unguarded expression on his face. She was quite unable to read its meaning. Perhaps he was not even thinking about her, because although he was looking at her he seemed, as he had seemed at the service station yesterday, not to be really seeing her.

She reached the duty room, thankful that neither of her nurses had witnessed her encounter with Dr Travis, and that she had time to cool down and compose herself, alone. She charted Davey's medication and settled down to read the report, as she had planned, earlier, to do. She found she had to force herself to concentrate on the words on the page.

That day Kerry learned something of the loneliness of rank. In her training days she would have found time, over bedpans or meal trolleys, to pour out her troubles in the ear of a sympathetic nurse. They would have commiserated with her and laughed over it together and she would have felt better. But she could scarcely weep on the shoulder of one of her nurses, even had she wanted anyone else to know what had happened. She just wanted to forget it as quickly as possible.

The day that she had looked forward to so eagerly

dragged by. She kept herself busy, although even that was not easy. This was a hospital where parents were encouraged to spend as much time with their children as possible, and it took many of the nursing duties off the staff's shoulders.

She got to know the children and talked to parents who there, encouraging them to discuss their worries with her. She explored the contents of cupboards, treatment room, trolleys. She gavaged a wee tot in a humidicrib.

Remembering Sister Dutton's hint to 'keep behind' Nurse Baker, she walked quietly up and stood on the other side of the bed as Nurse Baker prepared to change the dressing of five-year-old Tammy, who had a central venous catheter inserted for continuous infusion of her medication. Kerry said, 'Go ahead, Nurse,' then spoke cheerfully to Tammy, who appeared quite unperturbed about the procedure. Kerry watched as Baker, masked and gloved, carefully removed the sterile cover from the trolley beside the bed. She cast an expert glance over its contents. Everything was there, even to the plastic bag tied on the end to receive dirty dressings and swabs.

Baker seemed a little nervous about proceeding in Sister's presence, so Kerry continued to talk to Tammy, appearing not too absorbed in what Baker was doing. But she was not so absorbed that she did not see Baker, having removed the dirty dressing from the catheter site and dropped it into the bag on the side of the trolley, reach for a swab with the same pair of forceps.

'Clean forceps, Nurse!'

Nurse flushed. 'Yes, Sister.' Dropping the used forceps, too, into the bag, she picked up a sterile pair and, with a slightly shaking hand, grasped a swab with the forceps and dipped it into the antiseptic lotion, with which she carefully cleaned around the catheter exit site.

From there, the procedure went flawlessly, and when it was completed and Baker had made her patient comfortable, Kerry felt justified in saying, 'Well done, Nurse,' in spite of the early slight imperfection.

'Thank you, Sister.' Nurse Baker turned to wheel her trolley out of the ward, and Kerry smiled to herself. She could almost see the relief in Nurse Baker's back.

Kerry made a mental note to suggest the use of white plastic disposable forceps for use with dirty dressings. For one thing, they were clearly distinguishable from the metal ones and served as a reminder to the nurses to discard them before proceeding to the sterile part of the dressing. But she would wait until she was not quite such a new broom before making any suggestions.

Baker must have passed on a favourable report of the new Sister to Nurse Snow because, later, when the patients were settled and there was a lull in nursing duties, Snow came to Kerry and asked permission to use the time to practise setting up a trolley for a thoracocentesis, as she had a practical examination the following day. When Kerry had given her permission, Nurse Snow added shyly, 'Would you have time to supervise the setting, please, Sister?'

Kerry agreed gladly, and by the time the practice session was over, she felt that she had established a good rapport with both nurses.

At settling time, she caught a wistful look on Davey's face as he watched a bed being made up beside Lindy, whose mother was spending the night with her. Kerry asked, 'Would you like me to read you a story, Davey?' His usually sober little face lit up and he nodded quickly, several times. He chose a book from a pile on his table, and Kerry sat beside him on the bed and put an arm behind his back. He gave a sigh of pure contentment and snuggled against her. The small, confiding gesture gave her a surge of joy, and the contentment of the few minutes as she read to him almost compensated for the bad time his father had given her earlier.

Even so, she was relieved when she could finally hand over to the night staff, take her cape from its hook behind the door and leave the ward.

Outside, she stood for a moment, draping her cape around her shoulders and taking deep breaths of the crisply cool air which was as heady as wine after the controlled temperature inside the hospital.

As she entered the Nurses' Home, voices and laughter were coming from the Sisters' lounge at the top of the stairs, but she managed to reach her room without meeting anyone.

Shutting the door, she slipped out of her uniform and into a deep blue velour dressing gown. She plumped pillows on the bed and propped herself against them, with her knees folded beneath her chin and arms clasped around them. In solitude, she would think about her situation and try to get it all into perspective.

What was it going to mean to her future at Mount Myall that she had, so soon, fallen foul of the hospital's senior surgeon? To what extent did that offset the positive things about the hospital—the warmth of the staff, the modern, comfortable quarters, the well equipped and efficiently run wards? Added to that was the rapport she already had with Jo and the instantaneous bond she felt with Davey. Both of these brought a warm glow to her heart.

But the thought of Davey also led to thoughts of his father and she heard, again, a cold, hard voice accusing her of dereliction of duty. She, Kerry Martyn, to be accused of derelection of duty, to be made to feel inefficient and incompetent! It was too much! Her objectivity collapsed in a heap and the tears she had been keeping at bay for hours burned in her eyes and tightened her throat.

But tears and despair were foreign to her optimistic temperament and did not last more than a minute or two. Problems were there to be solved and challenges kept life interesting. She had been at the hospital for one day and already was thinking of quitting? Simply because one doctor had been hostile towards her? Shame!

She reminded herself that a nurse was liable to encounter, on occasions, a certain doctor or a certain Sister whom, try as she might, she could not please. The only way to survive such a situation was to say, 'Yes Doctor,' 'Yes, Sister', philosophically, and then go about her work to the best of her ability.

She would have to be prepared for this eventuality with Dr Travis, yet she instinctively felt there was a reason for his animosity. And if there *were* a reason for it, then it must be remediable. All she had to do was to find it.

The incident in the car? He had been justified in feeling frustrated at the time—she could forgive him that. But to carry it over to the next day so implacably? He would have to be a very egotistical and immature man to behave so. She did not want to believe that of him.

Perhaps he was overworked and overtired, or had had a bad day? No. She had seen that often enough in a doctor to be able to diagnose it fairly accurately.

Perhaps he thought a girl could only be a good nurse if she were a Plain Jane, four-square of stature and thirty years old? If so, that was *his* problem. She couldn't help it if she didn't fit his statistics and specifications. If he were concerned about her competence as a nurse, he had only to request Matron to see her reports and references. They were from one of the foremost hospitals in Australia and

Kerry knew he would find nothing in them of which she need be ashamed.

The more she thought about it, the more convinced she was that his hostility was directed against her, personally. Without in the least understanding why, she had the strange, chilling feeling that he did not want her in the hospital—that he was trying to drive her away.

She did not follow that train of thought very far before deciding that she was being irrational. She must not allow herself to become paranoid about the situation. The most constructive thing she could do was to find out more about the man. That should not be difficult in a hospital, where everyone knew all about everyone else. Was he a widower? A divorcee? Had his wife died in childbirth? Who was the woman in the car yesterday? It should be possible to get answers to these questions without divulging her motivation for asking them.

Even if she did not find the reason for his hostility, knowing more about him would help avoid pitfalls such as she had fallen into today. And also, she told herself, she could care for Davey more effectively if she knew more about his background. Asthma often had an emotional component somewhere in its aetiology.

In the meantime, her attitude towards Dr Travis would be that of cool professionalism. She was thankful she had managed to maintain a more or less unruffled front in his presence today.

By the time she had reached this stage in her thinking, her eyes were shining. She was relishing the thought of the campaign ahead of her, to win Dr Travis's respect and break down his prejudice against her.

She stood up and began to prepare for bed. As she slipped a creamy silk nightgown over her head, she visualised her next meetintg with Dr Travis, and found she was looking forward to it instead of dreading it.

It would be the first step in a process which would end with the good doctor eating humble pie.

And that, thought Kerry as she laid her head on her pillow, was a consummation devoutly to be wished.

CHAPTER THREE

KERRY woke next morning to the sounds of the a.m. shift preparing for duty. There was a sleepy greeting or two outside her door, a burst of stifled laughter, the distant running of showers. She lay thinking how good it was to be part of hospital life again. Three months away from it had been far too long.

In a tree outside her open window a magpie warbled joyfully. Another joined in and they sang together in carefree, contrapuntal harmony. When they stopped Kerry realised, for the first time, that here there was no constant background hum of traffic, as there had been in Sydney, just a silence that stretched to the hills and the bushland.

Everything about Mount Myall was so very nearly perfect. If only . . .! she thought, and then mentally chastised herself. 'If only' would accomplish nothing. Today was the day she tackled her problem. She pushed back the blankets purposefully and stood up. She showered and washed her hair, then, with a towel wrapped around her head, followed the aroma of brewed coffee to a small kitchen at the end of the corridor. It seemed overcrowded already, with three girls, also in dressing gowns, preparing snacks. Jo was one of them. She smiled at Kerry as she popped a slice of bread into a toaster.

'Hi! Shall I put one in for you?'

'Please.'

The other girls piled plates and mugs on to a tray and departed. Kerry spread butter and marmalade on the slice of toast Jo handed to her, poured coffee into a yellow mug and dropped thoughtfully into a chair beside the table. Perhaps fate had decided to be on her side this morning after doing all the wrong things yesterday. Jo had been at Mount Myall long enough to know most of its history. She would be able to answer Kerry's questions. More than that, Kerry was sure she could be trusted with a confidence, and decided to abandon her plan not to divulge her reasons for seeking information about Dr Travis, and confide the whole story to Jo.

'Are you busy this morning, Jo? Do you have time to talk?' she asked.

'I'm on days off and the only thing I'd planned to do is my washing, and that can keep. I've been wondering how your first day went.' Jo glanced at Kerry, then looked again, more keenly. 'Judging by that serious face, I'd say it hadn't gone so well. I hope you're not going to tell me you don't like us and plan to hotfoot it back to Sydney?'

Kerry grinned ruefully. 'On the contrary, I like it very much and I certainly hope I'll be staying.'

She sipped her coffee, wondering how to begin, as Jo, curious, waited. With Jo, Kerry decided, a direct approach would be best.

'My problem is Dr Travis,' she said.

It was Jo's turn to grin.

'My dear! So soon? We're used to nurses falling for Simon, but—in one day?'

Kerry chuckled mirthlessly.

'There must be a side to Dr Travis that I haven't seen yet. He's quite failed to impress me with his charms – which isn't important. What *is* important is that I've quite failed to impress him with mine. He seems to have a classical case of hate at first sight.'

'You're not serious?' Jo's eyes scanned Kerry's face incredulously. 'Yes, you are! But you must be mistaken.

That doesn't sound like Simon.' Jo was patently at a loss. 'Even if you *were* quite devoid of charms, which you're not, what could you have possibly done in the course of one day to make him dislike you?'

'You wouldn't believe! In two days, actually, because we met, you might say, the day before yesterday, before I'd even arrived here. That was the story I said I'd tell you about when we had time.'

Kerry recounted the story of the Mercedes man, and then of their encounter in the ward on the following day. When she had finished, Jo was silent, her fingers curled round her coffee cup, apparently absorbed in contemplation of its turgid brown contents, which she was slowly swirling.

'I heard that Davey was brought in with a bad attack of asthma the day before yesterday,' she said at last. 'Simon was probably hurrying to the hospital to him when you saw him on the road. He adores that child, you know.'

It was Kerry's turn to stare in disbelief.

'I keep wondering whether we're talking about the same man. If he's an adoring father, I'm Florence Nightingale! He didn't even seem to know how to talk to Davey yesterday. And Davey certainly didn't behave like a child who was thrilled to see his father. He obviously has emotional problems. I even found myself wondering whether it could be a case of child abuse.'

'Never!'

Jo put down her cup abruptly, and stood up. Kerry wondered whether their conversation was over so soon, whether her last statement had offended Jo, who obviously had a very high opinion of Dr Travis. But that was not so.

'Kerry,' Jo said, 'there's a lot more behind this that you realise, but I think you should be told. It's a long story, so pour yourself another cuppa and come to my room so we won't be interrupted—and so I can put my aching feet up. We had one helluva day in OR yesterday.'

Intrigued, Kerry followed her to her room. Jo waved a hand at the armchair and flopped on to the bed. Kerry ruffled her drying hair with her fingers in front of the mirror and then sat down. She was very curious to hear what Jo had to say, that she was looking so serious about.

Jo began slowly, consideringly.

'I'm sorry you've gained such a bad impression of Simon Travis. I just can't understand how it can have happened, even taking into account the circumstances of your first meeting with him. He's not at all like you think he is. He's a very skilled and dedicated doctor and a wonderful man. Once you've worked with him you'll know why we all think so much of him.'

Kerry shrugged her shoulders.

'If I get a chance to work with him. The way he feels about me, he'll probably tell Matron he'd rather not have me on his cases.'

'I doubt it. He appreciates a good nurse, and from all reports you're that. Just give him time and I'm sure he'll come to appreciate you.'

Remembering her resolve of the previous night, to make him change his mind about her, Kerry said a silent 'Amen' to that.

Jo plunged on into her story.

'Two years ago Simon lost his wife, Lori, in a tragic accident.'

Kerry gave a horrified gasp, her hand going to her mouth.

'Oh, dear! If only I'd known! No wonder he was so curt when I asked Davey about his mother.'

'That was unfortunate, but you had no way of knowing. Anyway, he's used to that kind of thing by now and I can't believe he'd hold it against you. Anyway, to continue . . . Simon was driving, with Lori in the passenger seat, at the time of the accident. Their car was forced off the road by a semi-trailer and hit a stobie pole. It wasn't Simon's fault—the court eventually threw the book at the driver of the semi. Lori was badly injured, but Simon wasn't really hurt—just shaken. Lori had to have emergency surgery, and Simon was the only surgeon at the hospital at the time who was qualified to do it. There was nothing wrong with the surgery—Simon was superb under the circumstances, but Lori died on the table.'

A long 'Pheew!' escaped Kerry's lips. 'How ghastly!'

'It was! I was in theatre, scrubbed, at the time, and I'll never forget it. Lori went into hypovolemic shock and there was nothing Simon or any of us could do that would reverse it. He was utterly devastated—we all were. I never want to live through a few minutes like that again. It was the very worst experience of all my nursing days.'

Jo was silent, sober-faced, remembering. Then she went on.

'There had to be a coroner's inquest, of course, because Lori had died on the table. Simon stayed for that and then he went away—nobody quite knew where—we did hear he was in Greece for a time. No one expected him to come back to work in the hospital, but he did, eventually, after about six months.'

'Why did he come back?' asked Kerry. 'Surely it would have been easier for him to have started life over, somewhere else?'

'He's never talked about it, at least not with any member of the staff, as far as I know. Perhaps he felt he'd run away for long enough and that he had to work through his grief here, where it happened. Also, Mount Myall is his home town. His family has lived here for generations. If he hadn't come back then, he might never have at all. And then there was Davey.'

'Yes, of course. What about Davey? What happened to him while his father was away? He would have been—how old, three or four?' queried Kerry.

'Almost four. An aunt of Simon's came to look after him. She's still there. She's a kind soul, elderly and single, but without much idea of how to handle a small boy, especially one with Davey's problems. She tries hard, but she's pathetically lacking in self-confidence.'

'Which Davey is probably aware of and which would add to his own sense of insecurity. Poor child!'

'Yes. It was only after Simon came back that David began to get asthma. Several doctors have investigated it and they all say it's emotionally triggered. The tragic thing about it is that it seems to be his father who triggers it. Davey's bad attacks all occur after he's been with Simon.'

'*Every* time he sees his father?' Kerry queried. 'Because if that's so, it means that either he has very frequent attacks or he doesn't see his father very often.'

'Simon *is* very busy, and I don't suppose he sees all that much of Davey,' Jo told her.

Kerry was gradually realising the implications of all she had heard and feeling very sorry for Davey.

'It must have been frightfully traumatic for the child,' she said 'To lose his mother, like that, and then his father too, for six months. Six months seems to be for ever at that age.'

Kerry realised she was clutching a cold, empty coffee cup, and leaned forward to place it on Jo's dressing table.

'Davey might even have thought that his father was responsible for his mother's death, in some way. Kids are pretty quick to pick up things like that. Perhaps that's the cause of his emotional reaction to his father. Or maybe he hadn't realised that she was gone for ever and he expected her to come back when his father did. And when his father did return, alone, he was too engrossed in his own grief to be aware that there was a small child who was grieving too, and who needed him.'

Kerry paused and shook her head slowly. 'It's no wonder Davey had problems. I'm so glad you told me all this, Jo. It will help me to understand the poor kid while he's in my care. Perhaps I can do something to help him.'

'The reason I told you was that I hoped it would help you to understand *Simon*,' said Jo.

'It has, too. But he's an adult and a doctor. He must have all the answers about how to handle grief. If his reaction towards me is any indication, then I'd say he's not handling it very well, because he's still getting much too upset over trifles. I hope that doesn't sound unsympathetic. I'm not, really, and I *will* make an effort to revise my first impressions of Dr Travis in the light of what I now know about him.'

Although she had been so engrossed in Jo's story, Kerry had been half conscious of a thought niggling at her mind, and now she allowed it so surface.

'Actually, Jo,' she said, 'I can't see anything in all this that explains Dr Travis's attitude towards me, personally, Apart from my comment to Davey about his mother, it all seems rather irrelevant, and that was my very last *faux pas,* so it couldn't have been that that made him take such an instant dislike to me.'

It was Jo's turn to consider.

'I can't explain it to you either, Kerry, but don't judge him too quickly. He does have times when he seems tense and unusually quiet, but I've never known him to take it out on a member of the staff.'

'That's nice for the rest of the staff,' said Kerry, a little sarcastically, 'but not very complimentary to me. I wonder what I've got that they haven't?'

Jo gave her an odd look. She opened her mouth as though she were going to say something, then closed it and turned to gaze out of the window, as though seeing something a long way off. After a moment or two Kerry gave an uneasy half-laugh.

'Jo, you're not psychic, are you? You look for all the world like someone who's dipping into the future and is of two minds whether you like what you see.'

Jo came back with a laugh. 'That's me! Josephine Nostradamus! Sees all, knows all!'

That seemed to be the end of that line of conversation, but another thought occurred to Kerry. 'You haven't told me who was the *grande dame* in Dr Travis's car that day.'

Jo chuckled at the description. 'That, without a doubt, would be Alicia Holmes.'

'Is she likely to be the happy ending of your Simon's story?'

'Heaven forbid! Though Alicia would like to think so. She's an old friend of the family, posing as comforter. Everyone but Simon knows that her intentions are strictly unplatonic.'

'Jo! Your claws are showing. I didn't know you could be . . .'

'Bitchy? Where Alicia Holmes is concerned I can be worse than that. It's not just that she has designs on Simon that wouldn't be good for him. It's her attitude towards us lowly creatures at the hospital. She belongs to one of the town's wealthiest families, and give her her due, she's a very good fund-raiser for the hospital. She's even on the Board. But that's about as close as she likes to get. When she's near patients she behaves as though she's afraid to breathe, in case she catches something. And I'm sure she'd like to make a rule that we nurses all carbolise ourselves in Dettol before we mingle with the worthy citizens of the town.'

'Sounds like a lovely lady. *Do* we mingle with the citizenry?'

'Yes, quite freely. It's a friendly town and very supportive of the hospital. Quite a few of our nurses have married and settled down here. A number of our trainees are local lasses, though most of them tend to migrate to Canberra or Sydney once they graduate. You know—the grass is always greener . . .'

'They might find it's not. You really have a superb hospital. I'm impressed.'

'That, from a connoisseur! Thanks,' laughed Jo. 'Actually, we owe a lot of it to the town. People here have a great deal of civic pride, and also money. One of the ways we acknowledge their support is by giving a Hospital Ball each year. It's coming up soon, and if you go, you'll have a chance to meet the townsfolk. It's really quite fun. The goodwill flows, along with the punch.'

'I'll look forward to it—always supposing I'm still here. Dr Travis and Alicia Holmes sound like a powerful combination. They may have had me run out of town before then, if I continue as I've begun.'

'Nonsense! My crystal ball tells me you have a long and happy future at Mount Myall.'

'Then I hope your crystal ball is accurate. And thanks, Jo, for telling me your story, even though it leaves me where I was last night—convinced that Dr Travis thinks I'm too young for the job. I'll just have to prove him wrong.'

Jo put in a last word on Dr Travis's behalf. 'You must believe, Kerry, that Simon really does love Davey. There's absolutely nothing he wouldn't do if it would help Davey, physically or emotionally.'

When Kerry had gone. Jo remained on the bed, deep in thought. After a few moments she gave a small nod of her head and murmured, 'Who knows? It might work. It just might work.'

Back in her own room, Kerry was feeling a little battered, and not for herself this time. Dr Travis's story had affected her deeply. When she had first seen him she thought she had seen tragedy in his eyes. Yesterday, there had been only hostility. Could the two be somehow connected? No, that was not possible. He had never even laid eyes on her until two days ago.

And Jo? Where did Jo fit into all this? She had been almost defensive about Dr Travis and had told his story with sensitivity and compassion. That, alone, would not have surprised Kerry, because it was in keeping with the kind of person she judged Jo to be. What *was* out of character was the depth of Jo's dislike of Alicia Holmes. Was Jo jealous? Was she a little bit—even more than a little bit—in love with Dr Travis? If she were, and if it ever worked out, Kerry was inclined to think that it was a fate better than Simon Travis deserved. But then did he really deserve Alicia Holmes, if she were half as unpleasant as Jo had indicated? It would be most interesting to meet the lady and judge for herself.

Jo? Or Alicia? As Kerry took a fresh uniform from her wardrobe and dressed for her second day on duty, she did not feel overjoyed about the idea of either of them being Simon Travis's consolation. She did not stop to ask herself why.

When Kerry arrived on the ward that afternoon, Sister Dutton's greeting was so enthusiastic that Kerry wondered whether Jo had already co-opted her into making her feel more positive about the hospital and her future there.

But Sister went on, 'Davey has pestered every nurse he's seen this morning, asking whether you're here yet. He's usually such a quiet little boy. What did you do to make such an impression on him?'

'I can't imagine. I read him a bedtime story . . .'

'We've all done that from time to time without him falling head over heels in love with us!'

Kerry was somewhat embarrassed, though pleased.

'He's a dear little boy. I hope he hasn't been upset?'

'On the contrary. He slept like a lamb last night and Doctor has reduced his medication to six-hourly today.'

'That's good,' said Kerry and, without thinking, added, 'I wish I could have made a good impression on his father too.'

'What do you mean by that?' Sister's sharp eyes looked at Kerry keenly.

Not wanting to have the saga of her clashes with Dr Travis known throughout the hospital, Kerry laughed and said easily, 'Dr Travis came in yesterday, just after you left, and was not at all impressed that I didn't know when Davey had last had Ventolin.'

Sister's 'Oh' conveyed 'Is that all?' and she turned to her report. 'Well, we'd better get on with it. Dr Travis is reducing a fractured tib and fib on a lad called Terry White, ten years old, and they should be here any time. There's a fracture bed ready next to Davey—they can be company for each other. Nurse Baker can watch Terry till he's fully conscious.'

Just as the handing-over was finished, the small entourage arrived from Theatre, and although she was officially off duty now, Sister Dutton accompanied Kerry to the ward. Kerry hoped it was not a vote of no-confidence in herself, that Sister had stayed on.

Dr Travis was there, standing apart from the group while the small unconscious form was transferred from trolley to bed. Then he moved across to adjust the weight that would provide traction on Terry's fractured leg. Another, younger doctor, obviously the anaesthetist, stood watching. Both doctors were still in dark green theatre gowns and caps, with masks hanging loosely about their necks. They had the flaccid, heavy-eyed look that told of a long morning in surgery.

Davey sat up with an expectant smile when he saw Kerry. She returned his smile but put a finger to her lips to warn him to be quiet for the time being. If Dr Travis saw the small exchange, he gave no sign. He did not speak to either Davey or Kerry but, rather pointedly, addressed Sister Dutton.

'It was quite a nasty fracture, Sister, but seems, on X-ray, to have reduced nicely.'

Sister said firmly, 'Sister Martyn is in charge this afternoon, Doctor, so I'm sure Terry will be in good hands.'

With a flash of understanding and gratitude, Kerry saw why Sister Dutton had stayed on. She was as kind as she was shrewd. She was there to smooth the way, if there were any reason to do so, and to express her confidence in Kerry to Dr Travis. Bless you, thought Kerry.

Dr Travis glanced briefly at Kerry, then turned his attention to the weights again, rather unnecessarily, Kerry thought, as they seemed to be nicely adjusted already. Watching him, she felt a surge of pity, but then she hardened her heart. Her own *cause célèbre* had nothing to do with his past history, however tragic that might have been.

Sister Dutton's remark had given the younger doctor the opportunity he had obviously been waiting for, and he turned towards Kerry with a wide, boyish smile, saying, 'I haven't met our new Sister yet. Isn't somebody going to introduce us?'

His easy charm and friendliness were so refreshing, compared with Dr Travis's persisting coolness, that Kerry responded to Sister Dutton's introduction of Dr Peter Treloar with more warmth than she might otherwise have done. Peter Treloar would have continued the exchange of pleasantries with Kerry, but Dr Travis cast a quelling glance in their direction and Peter hastily took the chart which Sister Dutton was holding out to him, and began making notes on it, at the same time giving verbal instructions about pain relief for Terry.

Dr Travis peeled off his green cap, flicked the mask to the back of his neck so he could untie the strings under his chin, then began fumbling with one hand behind his back for the ties of his gown. Kerry was standing nearby, feeling rather superfluous, and, trained to the concept that the nurse is handmaid to the surgeon, she stepped behind him and, with a practised flick-flick, loosened the two ties of the gown. Dr Travis looked surprised, said, 'Thank you', slipped the gown off and expertly rolled it into a ball, inside out, with cap and mask inside. He looked round vaguely, as though wondering what to do with this bundle, met Kerry's eye, which had a tiny twinkle in it, and passed the bundle into her outstretched hand. It was the kind of small charade that doctors and nurses act out constantly—the helpless doctor, the willing, ever-watchful nurse—yet he seemed curiously ill at ease as he turned away to wash his hands, before moving over to Davey's bedside.

Peter Treloar slapped Terry gently on the cheek, saying, 'Wake up, mate,' lifted one heavy eyelid, said, 'He'll do,' and departed with a cheerful, all embracing wave.

Kerry said, 'I'll stay with Terry, Sister, if you'll send Nurse Baker in, please,' and Sister Dutton also departed. Kerry drew the curtain between Terry's and Davey's beds, to give Dr Travis a semblance of privacy as he visited with his son. Her cheeks flamed as she heard Davey, who probably considered the screen as good as a wall between them, say to his father, 'Did you see the nurse with the pretty smile? She's going to get me a book about Winnie the Pooh.'

Kerry thought she knew at least part of the reason for her popularity with Davey, but her cheeks were still flushed when, Nurse Baker having arrived to take over care of Terry, she had no option but to step from behind the screen. To Davey's eager, 'Hullo, Sister,' she said quickly, 'I'll see you later, Davey. I'm busy now,' and made her escape, but not without first seeing Dr Travis raise one dark sarcastic eyebrow. His meaning was clear. That abominable man thinks I'm trying to curry favour with him by making up to his son, she thought. He couldn't be more wrong. There's just one reason I want to make a good impression on Dr Travis, and that's to throw in his teeth his first assessment of me. I would never make Davey a pawn in that game. I'm concerned about Davey and I shall do what's best for him, whatever his father thinks. And I refuse, I utterly refuse, to let that man upset me.

But she wondered, as she took her pen from her pocket to make some notes on Terry's chart, how it could be that she and Davey had such instant rapport, while she and his father, from the very beginning, had had only animosity towards one another.

CHAPTER FOUR

'GOOD MORNING, Sister Martyn. Do you accept lifts from strange doctors?'

Kerry had just left the hospital grounds and was stepping out briskly to walk into town. It was a mild cloudless spring morning and she had rolled her slim white pants up to just below her knees, showing her tanned legs and feet in pink moccasins. Her deep pink shirt was open at the neck and her hair swung, free and shining, to her shoulders.

She turned at the sound of the voice, to see Peter Treloar smiling at her from behind the wheel of a cheeky red Porsche. His hair, which had been mostly hidden by the theatre cap yesterday, was not quite as red as the car, but it was unmistakably auburn, and thick and curly. His eyes, crinkled by his smile, were surveying her frankly, his scrutiny was so openly appreciative that she could not be offended by it.

She laughed. 'It depends on how strange the doctor is.'

Peter said pleadingly, '*Almost* normal.'

Kerry ran her gaze admiringly over his car and said, 'How could I refuse? She's beautiful!'

Peter beamed with pride and got out to open the door for her. When he was settled behind the wheel again, he gave an exaggerated sigh and said mournfully, 'So much for my fatal charm! One day I'll find a lady who'll love me for myself alone!'

Kerry chuckled. 'The lady might just demand that you love her more than you do your car. And then where would you be?'

'Sunk! But tell me, where are you going to, my pretty maid, on this lovely morning which is getting better by the minute?'

'I'm going a-shopping, sir. I *was* also going a-walking—for the good of my health and to take in the local scenery. You see how weak-willed I am when it comes to physical exertion.'

'You look the picture of health to me and I'm sure you get enough exercise pounding the wards every day. What the doctor prescribes for you this morning is some congenial company and a guide who knows every beauty spot in town.'

'I'll bet you do!' retorted Kerry.

Peter looked sideways at her and grinned.

The car had been running gently down a long, tree-lined street and was already approaching the centre of the town. Peter cruised slowly until he found a place to park, then pulled into the kerb. Kerry was sorry that their meeting had been so brief. She had enjoyed Peter's company for those few minutes. As he held the door for her, she said, 'Thanks for the lift, Peter. Could you point me in the direction of a bookshop? Or don't they figure in your guide book?'

'Certainly. But not so fast! I haven't shown you a single local feature yet. Allow me to point out the best little coffee shoppe in town, outside of which we just happen to be standing.'

'It certainly is very convenient. You seem determined to wreck all my good resolutions this morning. But why not?'

They entered the dim, fragrant interior and found a secluded table in a corner farthest from the door. Over steaming cups of cappuccino and buttered croissants, they chatted casually, with a growing sense of camaraderie. Peter, Kerry learned, was from Adelaide.

'Culture,' she said, and, in reply to his enquiring look, she added, 'Over here we tend to think of South Australians as flitting from art shows to operas to symphony concerts.'

'Oh, dear! Now I have to let the side down by admitting I've never been to one such. You wouldn't settle for Aussie Rules football, surfing or pub crawling?'

'Philistine! But I'd settle for surfing, any day.'

'Ha! You're an enthusiast! But you're a long way from surfing beaches here. You're a Sydney-sider?' queried Peter.

'Actually, my home is in Cairns, so I've always lived near the sea. Except for a year I spent in Europe.'

'What were you doing there for a year? Nursing?'

'No. It was before I went nursing. I was mostly getting my head on straight. I had no idea, when I left school, what I wanted to do. I thought it would be a choice between music and art, and Daddy said he'd stand me a year in Europe to find out which I really wanted to build my life around. I've wondered, since, whether he wanted me to find out for myself that my little talents didn't really stack up so well outside of our rather limited circle. But I had a marvellous time, browsing round art schools, galleries, going to concerts. I've never regretted that year and I've always been grateful to Daddy for giving it to me.'

'And?'

'And I came back as unsure as when I went of what I wanted to do with my life. To fill in time, I took a job as a nurse assistant in a local hospital. And that was it! Nursing! It was there waiting for me all the time and I'd never even considered it as a career.'

'And you've never regretted going into nursing?' he asked.

'Oh, no! Have *you* ever regretted going into medicine?'

'I won't say there haven't been moments when I've wondered what it would be like to have a nine-to-five job and never be called out in the middle of the night.'

'Haven't we all!' laughed Kerry.

'So what made you choose Mount Myall, having nursed in Sydney?'

'I was offered a position in theatres when I'd finished training. But for one thing, I like my patients conscious and for another, I enjoy clinical nursing, not spending fifty per cent of my time filling in forms and all the other red tape that goes with being a charge Sister in a big hospital. And I think it's good to diversify—to see what nursing is like in a different sort of hospital. My only regret about Mount Myall is that it's so far from the sea. I'm really going to miss that.'

'Plenty of people here have pools, though I admit that's not the same as a good surfing beach.'

Peter broke off suddenly, his gaze fixed on the door.

'What do you know! There's the Boss.'

Peter's voice is as revealing as his face, thought Kerry. There was respect, even awe, in the way he said, 'The Boss.'

Following the direction of his eyes, she was not surprised to see that it was Dr Travis who was entering the coffee shop.

'He's on his own,' said Peter. 'Do you mind if we ask him to join us?' He half rose, as though her consent was a foregone conclusion.

She said quickly, 'Please don't!' Peter looked at her in surprise and she added lamely, 'He's probably meeting someone.'

Dr Travis was seating himself at a table a little distance away. He was facing more or less in their direction and Kerry shrank back into the shadows, hoping he had not seen them, a manoeuvre that was not lost on Peter. He was watching her in some bewilderment and she guessed she owed him an explanation, though not a full one—she would make it a very simplified version of the state of affairs between herself and Dr Travis.

'Don't get the idea that I'm shy of meeting doctors socially, Peter. It's just that your "Boss" seems to have taken an instant dislike to me and he probably wouldn't enjoy his coffee one bit, in my presence.'

'You're not serious? That doesn't sound like the Boss.'

'And you sound just like Jo,' said Kerry crossly. 'I seem to be the only person in Mount Myall who doesn't see Dr Travis through rose-coloured spectacles. I've found him rude and overbearing.'

Peter shook his head as though he could not believe what he was hearing, but he sat down, obviously deciding that the subject of Dr Travis was a touchy one and not to be pursued. Instead he said, 'So you've met Jo. Now *there's* a broth of a girl.'

'At least we agree on that.'

'Jo got me over a rocky spot when I first came here as a raw young anaesthetist, that I've never forgotten. And she did it so tactfully that no one else even noticed how nearly I'd blotted my copy book. I'd made the most elementary, unforgivable blue in the book—failed to check a patient's name tag and case notes in theatre, and was about to render unconscious a middle-aged lady who was there to have a lipoma removed under local anaesthesia. I'd mistaken her for a cholecystectomy who was also on the list—also female and also middle-aged. Jo saw what I was up to and made some comment to her scrub nurse which brought me up with a jolt but which no one else noticed was for my benefit. I've been eternally grateful to Jo. Some Sisters would have taken a delight in seeing a young doctor cut down to size, but not Jo. I have a lot of time for that young lady.'

His tone was so warm that Kerry thought, It's a pity Jo's sights are set on Dr Travis. She could do a lot worse than Peter Treloar.

She stood up. 'I really must go, Peter. Thanks so much. It's been nice.'

She moved towards the door, with Peter following. She avoided looking in Dr Travis's direction and assumed by the fact that Peter did not speak that he had done likewise—to avoid embarrassing her, probably. Thoughtful Peter! He really was a dear.

Standing on the footpath outside the shop, Peter said, 'I enjoyed that too, Kerry, although we didn't manage our guided tour.' He hesitated, thinking, then said, 'Would it be too forward of me, on so short an acquaintance, to ask you to be my partner for the Hospital Ball which is coming up in a few weeks' time?'

'I heard about it.' Kerry thought, it would be nice to have a partner lined up for the Ball. And all the more so if that partner were Peter. Although it was too early to make stipulations about keeping their relationship casual, she felt sure that would be all Peter wanted. She did have one reservation about the Ball.

'I'd be happy to go with you, Peter, as long as I wouldn't be treading on someone else's domain. Is there anybody who might be upset if I accept?'

Peter grinned, a little sheepishly. 'Not at the moment.'

'Just a trail of broken hearts?'

'That could be a compliment, or it could mean you suspect me of being a philanderer.'

'I don't know you well enough to suspect anything.'

'Then we'll have to remedy that—give me the chance to prove what a sterling, salt-of-the-earth guy I am. The Ball's a few weeks away yet—couldn't we fit in a movie in the meantime?'

'I'm going to be very occupied with my new job, Peter.

I'm not looking for too many social engagements.'

'Neither am I,' said Peter, then added pleadingly, 'Just one movie. We really should get to know one another better before the Ball.'

Kerry laughed. 'A fine attempt at rationalisation, Doctor! Just one movie, then.'

'Great! I'll be in touch when you know your roster for next week.'

Peter was standing facing the door of the coffee shop as they talked. Kerry's back was to it. She had forgotten Dr Travis was in the shop until Peter said 'Hullo' to someone emerging from it. She turned her head and was face to face with Dr Travis. He smiled and said pleasantly, 'Good morning, Sister. Be seeing you, Peter,' and turned and walked away down the street.

Peter looked at Kerry quizzically. There was no need for him to say what he was thinking. Kerry flushed a little and said, 'Now I suppose you think I've got an over-active imagination.'

'No. Just that it's early days yet to be deciding that someone doesn't like you.'

Kerry was silent. She did not want to tell Peter the story of her encounters with Dr Travis, even to defend herself against the criticism implicit in his last remark. And even if she did tell him, he would probably still think she was being over-sensitive.

Looking at her watch, she said, 'Is there a bookshop near here that sells children's books?'

'The newsagent one block down on the left stocks them.' Peter looked curious about her intended purchase, but she merely said, 'Thanks again for the coffee, Peter.' She walked on down the street, pondering over the last hour. She was happy that she had a new friend in Peter, happy with her invitation to the Ball, wondering why her impressions about Dr Travis were so contrary to everyone else's. Had she indeed been over-sensitive, as Peter thought? No! The animosity had been there—she had not imagined it. She could hope, though, and she could act on the assumption that it was a passing thing and that in the future he would be, with her, the nice guy that Jo and Peter thought him.

When she arrived on the ward that afternoon, Davey was so excited that he did not notice the parcel she held in her hand. Kerry was glad of that, because his father was sitting by the bed and she did not want to give the book to Davey in Dr Travis's presence. She was not yet confident enough of a change in his attitude to risk him misconstruing her gift to Davey.

'Sister Martyn, guess what! I'm allowed to go home tomorrow—and guess what!' Davey was bouncing with excitement.

'I'm not very good at guessing. You'll have to tell me.'

'Daddy says you can come and visit me. When can you come?'

He was so sure she would accept his invitation. Kerry glanced at Dr Travis, who was watching her quizzically. She was in a quandary. She did not want to disappoint Davey, but she knew that his father would put his own, unflattering interpretation on an acceptance. She prevaricated.

'Thank you for asking me, Davey. I'd love to come some day, but just now I'm very busy settling in here at the hospital, so I don't have time for visiting yet. Perhaps later on?'

Davey's face fell. He made no protest but shrank back on his pillows, looking away from them both. Kerry's heart smote her. He accepted disappointment much too readily, she thought, as if it was what he expected from adults. She desperately wanted to bring that eager look back to his face.

His father, too, was watching Davey and Kerry could read in his face displeasure on Davey's behalf at her refusal, but relief on his own. He also was in a dilemma. But his next words wiped out any stirring of sympathy she was beginning to feel for him.

'You seem to be a fast worker, Sister. Perhaps you could expedite your settling in a little. I have to fly to Canberra for a one-day surgeons' conference on Friday. Could you perhaps visit David some time then?'

How dared he! She knew he was referring to having seen her with Peter that morning. But he had done it so obliquely as to deny her the opportunity of defending herself or explaining that she had met Peter quite by accident. Then, adding insult to injury, he had implied that she was welcome in his home as long as he was not there. It was only Davey's presence that restrained her from giving vent to the anger she felt.

Davey was watching her with renewed hope, quite unaware of the tension in the air. Kerry felt helpless, manipulated into a corner.

'I'll come on Friday, then, Davey,' she said, and made her escape, still clutching her parcel.

She went to the pantry and poured herself a cup of strong coffee which she took back to the duty room, where she drew some papers towards her on the table so she would seem to be working. It took ten minutes for her indignation to subside and she thought, then, what price good resolutions? And what would Peter make of her latest encounter with the Boss if she told him of it? She had no shadow of doubt what lay behind Dr Travis's words. But, related to a third party, they could seem too nebulous to have justified her reaction. She sighed and resolved to say nothing to anyone about the incident. Except to tell Jo when she saw her about Davey's invitation, and also about Peter's, to the Ball.

* * *

On Thursday morning, Kerry put on jeans and walking shoes and, taking a sketching pad and pencil, set off along a track into the low hills behind the hospital. She spent two hours walking, or sitting on a log sketching, trying to catch the effect of sunshine filtering through the trees. It was warm and peaceful and very quiet.

When she returned, there were letters for her on the board in the foyer—a fat one from her sister-in-law, a card in Tony's illegible scrawl, and two pencilled messages. One said, 'Peter rang. Will call again.' About their movie date, no doubt.

The second message made her heart thump suddenly, for no reason that she cared to analyse. but she had to admit that it was a ridiculous reaction to a note that said, simply, 'Dr Travis rang. Will contact you later.' She knew why. He had managed to find some reason to cancel her visit tomorrow. She did not know whether to be glad or sorry.

As she stood with the notes in her hand, a rather stilted, unnatural voice behind her said, 'Oh, it's you, Sister Martyn. I see you got your messages.'

Kerry turned, to see a Sister whose name she could not recall. There was an odd little smile on the Sister's face and a curious note in her voice that Kerry could not interpret until she added, 'You *are* doing well for yourself. Phone calls from doctors already!'

Kerry had no time to reply before the other girl moved on. But, she reflected, she knew the type—a girl who put doctors in a class apart from ordinary mortals, who had never had a date with one herself and was inordinately jealous of anyone who had. Soon the whole staff would know about Kerry's phone calls. It was annoying, but there was nothing she could do about it, except see Jo soon, and explain about them to her herself.

It was difficult to concentrate on work that afternoon.

The ward was not busy and time passed slowly. Davey's bed was empty and Terry was lamenting at being left behind. He cheered up when Kerry told him he would soon be getting round the ward on crutches, like a wounded soldier. A tiny premature baby, several weeks old and only recently graduated from its humidicrib and gavage tube, and not at all interested in sucking a bottle to obtain his nourishment, had been transferred across from Maternity Wing, where there was a rush on. Kerry spent some time, every three hours, in patiently coaxing him to take his feeds. It was very peaceful in the nursery, warm and soporific. The other girls drifted in occasionally, to admire the tiny mite in Kerry's arms, and to chat about other patients.

Kerry was having her break, sipping tea and scanning through Davey's discharge summary in the duty room, when the phone rang. Nurse Snow, who was charting drugs in the duty room, answered it, said, 'Dr Travis, Sister,' handed Kerry the receiver and went on with her charting.

'Sister Martyn speaking.' Kerry kept her voice cool and controlled with an effort.

'Sister, this is Simon Travis. We have a small complication regarding your visit tomorrow.'

So she had been right—he was going to opt out. Her disappointment, she knew, was all for Davey. But the cool, precise voice continued, 'I'd forgotten that Friday is my aunt's morning for bridge and we can't interfere with that. But on Saturday, David and I have been invited to a barbecue and we wondered whether you would accompany us. There'll be no one of David's age there, and as he's so lately out of hospital, it would be a relief to have you there.'

Kerry's thoughts were chasing one another round her head. She was not at all sure she wanted to accompany father and son on a social outing, although the way the invitation was worded, she would be justified in charging a fee for her services! It was certainly something quite different from paying Davey a brief visit at his home, in his father's absence. But could she disappoint Davey, however uncomfortable an outing it might be for her?

She heard herself saying, 'Yes, I'm free. Saturday in my day off duty this week.'

'Then may we pick you up at your quarters at eleven?'

'I'll be ready. How has Davey been since he went home?'

'Very well. A quiet dy in the open air will do him good. Oh, Sister, there'll be horse riding in the afternoon. I mention it so you can be suitably attired, should you wish to ride.'

'Thank you, but I don't ride,' she told him.

'Goodbye until Saturday, then.'

'Goodbye.'

Kerry put down the receiver and sat still, slowly exhaling as she considered the implications of this new development. She realised that Nurse Snow was still in the room, concentrating hard on her charting, trying to look as if she were deaf, and probably feeling embarrassed that she had not left the room during what had turned out to be a personal conversation. She must be bursting with curiousity, and, discreet girl though she was, Kerry knew she would not be able to resist telling someone that the new Sister was dating Dr Travis. The news would spread through the hospital like wildfire. That must not be allowed to happen.

Kerry clasped her hands on the table to hide their slight tremulousness, and said, as matter-of-factly as she could,

'That was Dr Travis, Nurse.' Stupid of her—of course Nurse knew it was Dr Travis. 'Davey was very insistent before he left here that I should visit him at his home. Dr Travis was not at all keen on the idea, for some reason, but he gave in to Davey and I was to have gone tomorrow. Now it seems there are complications about tomorrow, so he's asked me to go with Davey to a barbecue somewhere in the country, on Saturday, instead.'

She could see that Nurse Snow was disappointed that she was not going to be the bearer of news of an exciting new hospital romance, but she accepted the explanation and merely said politely, 'I hope you have a good time, Sister. Give my love to Davey.'

Kerry was still not sure that she had been successful in forestalling gossip about herself and Dr Travis, so, later that evening, when she and Nurse Snow were sorting linen into bundles for the morning's bed-change, she casually mentioned that Peter Treloar had invited her to go with him to the Hospital Ball. The gleam of interest in Nurse Snow's eyes assured her that her red herring would pay off.

As soon as she was off duty, she went along to Jo's room. Jo was sitting up in bed, applying polish to her nails. She gave Kerry a quick glance, then returned to her task.

'Hullo. How's duty?' The greeting was restrained, and Kerry thought she knew why. She wished Jo felt confident enough in their friendship to confide in her her feelings for Simon Travis. That would come in time. In the meantime, she must convince Jo that there was nothing for her to worry about from Kerry herself. She plopped on to the end of the bed and launched into her account of the last day or two.

'I've been wanting to catch up with you, Jo, to fill you in on my ongoing saga with Dr Travis.'

'I heard you were going out with him and Davey on Saturday. You seem to have got over your initial hostility towards him very quickly. I'm glad. I really didn't expect it to last.' Jo sounded quite sincere. Kerry thought it best not to remind her that the 'initial hostility' had all been on Dr Travis's part.

She replied, 'I'm not sure it's anything more than an armed truce for Davey's benefit. You said, yourself, that Dr

Travis would do anything for Davey. I admit, he hasn't been too ungracious about it all, though he's made it very clear that I'll be there as a companion for Davey. He threw in a half-hearted invitation to ride, but he didn't exactly beat his breast when I refused.'

'Do you ride?' asked Jo.

'No, and I certainly don't plan to make my first attempt with Dr Travis looking on. I'd fall at his feet, for sure, and that's the last place I want to be.'

Jo laughed, quite merrily, and Kerry hoped she was getting across the message that nothing had really changed between herself and Simon Travis. Perhaps she could draw Jo out to talk about him.

'Is he a good rider?' she asked.

'Superb. It's his favourite relaxation these days. I don't recall that he and Lori rode much, if at all. They did a lot of entertaining. Lori was a terrific hostess, and they often had folk staying at the house.'

'Does he still live in the same house?'

'Yes. It's a big house on the other side of town. It used to be a very large property, but it's been subdivided as the town has grown in that direction. But the house is the same—big, rambling, comfortable. Lori had some lovely things in it, although one always felt that people were more important to her than things.'

They sat for a while in silence, Jo remembering, Kerry trying to fit Simon Travis into the background Jo had described, and feeling a certain curiosity to see it for herself. She would not have the opportunity, now that they were going to the barbecue, instead of to Davey's home.

Jo spoke first, quietly. 'I hear you've had another invitation too.'

This was safer ground. 'Yes, Peter Treloar. I'm really quite pleased about that one. He tells me he has no ties—no one who would be upset about him taking me to the Ball. I'll be very glad of his company for my first sortie into Mount Myall society.'

'Yes, of course.'

Jo still sounded subdued, as though, Kerry thought, she was having trouble dragging her thoughts away from the past and Lori. Or the present and Simon Travis? She made a further effort to distract her.

'Peter said you helped him a lot when he first came here, Jo. He was loud in his praises of you.'

Jo flushed slightly. 'He's a bright boy. He doesn't need help from anyone. Even though he's so young he's the town's only specialist anaesthetist and he's always busy. You'll be lucky to get through your date with him without being beeped.'

'That's a chance one always takes when one goes out with doctors.'

Jo opened her mouth as if to speak, then closed it again and blew gently on the nails of her right hand. Kerry's last words hung in the air between them, and she was uncomfortably aware that they gave the impression that she was used to dating doctors.

It had not been an easy conversation and, for the first time, Kerry was glad to say goodnight to Jo and escape to her room.

That was Thursday. On Friday, in the Home and on duty, she noticed an occasional curious glance her way, and she had to answer a leading question or two. But on the whole, Nurse Snow seemed to have done a good job, and most of the staff accepted that the outing on Saturday was all in the line of duty. Even Matron. Matron said, at tea on Friday evening, that she hoped it was a fine day for Kerry's outing tomorrow, and that she must tell her afterwards how she found Davey, as they had all become very fond of that young man.

CHAPTER FIVE

SIMON TRAVIS was punctual on Saturday morning and, for the first time, Kerry saw a glint of approval in his eyes as she came down the steps of the Nurses' Home towards him.

She had thought carefully about what to wear for this outing. She wanted to look nice yet unobtrusive—as befitted a companion for Davey. And she wanted to be dressed quite unsuitably for riding, should the question arise again. She had finally chosen a pale yellow figured Indian cotton skirt, nipped in at the waist and very full, and a snowy white cotton blouse with lace panels. She realised it made her look very young, but this morning she did not care. She *felt* young, and happy, and determined to enjoy her day out.

She ran lightly down the steps to the waiting car, smiling first at Simon Travis and then at Davey, who was bouncing up and down in the back seat. Kerry moved to join him there, but Simon was opening the front door for her and, not wishing to risk a confrontation, however small, so early in the day, she complied, though she would have felt much more at ease sitting with Davey.

Jo had said that Simon Travis rode superbly. Kerry had to admit that he looked superb in riding clothes. As he walked around the front of the car to resume his seat, she noted his breeches and fine leather riding boots, which revealed his lean, muscular strength. He was wearing a cream silk polo-necked sweater, and a dark brown cord riding jacket hung in the back of the car.

He had said, 'Good morning,' and smiled quite

pleasantly when she appeared. All he said now was, 'The weather's being kind to us,' then relapsed into silence. But it was not an unfriendly silence. He seemed relaxed, concentrating on driving and leaving her to chatter with Davey who, it was clear, had much he wanted to tell her.

Davey was sitting behind his father, and Kerry, half turned in her seat to see him as they talked, was acutely aware of the man at the wheel, of his strong, shapely surgeon's hands, of the fresh soap-and-aftershave smell of him. Without appearing to study him, she could see the clean line of his jaw and his mouth, which was, in repose, firm but not unkind. For one crazy second she allowed herself to wonder how it would feel to run her fingers through his thick, springy brown hair, but she quashed the thought and turned her head further so that he could see that her attention was wholly given to Davey.

Davey was talking eagerly about the characters in *Winnie the Pooh.* In the few days since she had given him the book, Tigger and Pooh Bear and Eeyore seemed to have become familiar and well-loved figures to him. Somebody must have spent quite some time reading the stories to him. His father?

Trying to imagine Simon Travis in that role, Kerry glanced at him. As though he had read her thoughts, he turned his head toward her slightly, with a half humorous, half sarcastic quirk of the lips and raising of an eyebrow that clearly said, Well? So what?

He was quick, much too quick, to guess what she was thinking. She would have to be more careful in future. Could he possibly also have known what she had been thinking, just a few moments ago? Her cheeks flaming at the thought, she turned quickly back to Davey.

Soon she saw that they were leaving the valley by the same road by which she had entered it—was it less than a week ago? It occurred to her for the first time that their destination could be Alicia Holmes' home. Alicia had been in the car with Simon Travis that day and they had been coming from the direction in which they were now heading.

As if in response of her thought, Davey said, 'We're going to Aunt Alicia's.' Kerry could not admit to any knowledge of Alicia Holmes, so she replied, 'Oh, you have an auntie? That's nice.'

'She's not my real auntie. She just told me to call her that.'

'Well, pretend aunties are nice too.'

'I suppose,' he said, with a marked lack of enthusiasm.

His father interposed, 'David is referring to Alicia Holmes. She's been a friend of our family for many years. She lives about twelve miles from town.' He was silent, following his own line of thought. Then he said, 'Have you never ridden, Sister?'

'I've never had the opportunity.'

'I suppose not.'

Kerry felt her hackles rise. He probably thought that she had no interests beyond the four walls of whatever nurses' home she happened to be living in. But, out of common courtesy, he could have asked what her interests were. Or where her home was. Or if she had any family. But he was probably too egotistical to think of asking such questions. Kerry reminded herself fiercely that she was here today as Davey's nurse-companion and, ignoring his father, she kept up a lively conversation with Davey over the back of her seat.

Soon they were turning off the road across a wide cattle grid and driving down a long avenue of poplars towards a house in the distance. The paddocks surrounding the house were as smooth and green as an English park. In the distance, a small herd of black and white cows grazed, looking as if they had been placed there for the sole purpose of enhancing the landscape. Nearer the house, several horses raised their heads as the car approached.

It was an idyllic scene, and as immaculate as Alicia Holmes herself had appeared, on the only occasion Kerry had seen her. She was looking forward with interest to meeting her now.

They followed the driveway past the house to where several cars and two or three horse floats were parked. On a broad expanse of lawn, in the shade of a copse of tall, white-trunked, lemon-scented gums, several men were gathered round a huge stone barbecue. Perhaps a dozen people stood in twos and threes, chatting, nearby.

Kerry stepped out of the car and waited as Simon Travis opened the luggage compartment and handed her a canvas bag. She could see in it a green frisbee, the handle of a small cricket bat and some books. Disjointed scraps of conversation reached her from the groups on the lawn, and she was suddenly shy about meeting these people. They obviously knew one another well and might be reticent about opening their ranks to a stranger. Then she realised that, to some extent, she had been prejudging them by what she had found Simon Travis to be. Country folk were known to be friendly, she reassured herself.

A figure detached itself from one of the groups and came towards them. Alicia Holmes, without a doubt. She was wearing jodhpurs and a creamy silk shirt, high at the neck with a big floppy tie and long sleeves. She was blonde, as Kerry remembered her, slim and tall and very lovely.

If a man were looking for beauty of face and figure, he need look no further than Alicia Holmes. But, thought Kerry, meeting Alicia's eyes for the first time, if he was looking for warmth and sincerity, he would not find them here. Simon Travis was watching Alicia, and it was very clear that it was beauty that interested him.

Alicia murmured, 'Darling,' and kissed him lightly and possessively on the cheek. 'And Davey!' Davey shrank away from the hand that was extended to deliver a pat on his head. 'Are you better now? I'm glad you didn't have to stay too long in that horrid hospital.' Not only the words but the high, stilted voice as Alicia talked down to Davey, grated on Kerry.

Alicia turned to Kerry. A puzzled look crossed her face as she said, 'How do you do,' to Simon Travis's introduction. 'Haven't we met somewhere before?'

Kerry had no intention of referring to the incident on the road, with Simon Travis looking on, so she simply said, 'I don't think so. I've only been a few days at Mount Myall Hospital.'

'And David has got to know you so well in such a short time? I hear he's taken quite a fancy to you.' Alicia's tone said, I can't imagine why.

Kerry said quietly, 'It would seem so.'

'Then you must both have a good time today. I see you've brought some things to amuse yourselves. That's good, because Simon and I will be rather busy.'

So saying, Alicia took Simon by the arm and led him away. Kerry had an absurd impulse to poke out her tongue at Alicia's departing back, like the child she had been treated as. But she laughed, determined to keep her sense of humour, and to enjoy her day, for Davey's sake, if for no other reason. Neither Simon Travis nor Alicia had made any attempt to introduce her to other guests, and the first move was not hers to make, so she began settling herself and Davey on the grass in a pleasant spot, not so isolated from the rest of the party as to make them conspicuous.

She need not have worried about being left alone. Almost immediately, a friendly older couple came across, introduced themselves and stayed to chat for several minutes. Davey was obviously a favourite with everyone, and a steady stream of people followed, so that their little encampment became a friendly enclave. Kerry responded wholeheartedly to the warmth and good fellowship. When the time came to eat, she and Davey were taken across to the tables, where they heaped their plates with steak and sausages, salads and condiments. Several times she caught Simon Travis looking in their direction, and was glad he could see for himself that they were managing very well, without any help from him.

It was some time after they had finished eating that he came across to them.

'Hullo, Daddy. Kerry has taught me a new game!' exclaimed Davey.

He raised his eyebrows. 'Kerry?'

'I told him to call me that,' she explained. 'I hope you don't mind.'

'Not at all. But it would be a little odd for me to continue calling you Sister. May I call you Kerry too?'

'Please do.' She wondered whether he would add, 'And please call me Simon,' but that did not seem to occur to him.

He said, 'We'll be riding for about an hour. Will you be all right for that time?'

'Of course.' Davey clearly had no doubts about it.

'You've been doing very well so far.'

'Yes, everybody has been most friendly. Just as I always expected country folk to be.' If he thought there was a reproof in her words, so be it.

He gave no sign that the barb had struck home, but stood looking down at them, his eyes going from one to the other. Most fathers would have sat down on the rug with them, but Simon always seemed to find it difficult to unbend with Davey—or was Kerry's presence inhibiting him? She had seen him at various times during the day in groups of people of which he seemed to be the life of the party. If only he would make more effort to get on with his son! It would take so little and mean so much to Davey.

She said, 'Davey would love to play battleships with you, if you could spare him the time.'

Again, the reproof was thinly veiled. He gave a lopsided half-smile which showed he had taken her point, but said, 'I can't stay now—the other riders are waiting. But afterwards, David, we will have a game.'

'Sure, Dad. That's OK.' Kerry was thrilled to hear the new confidence in Davey's voice.

An hour or so later the riders returned. Alicia was at Simon Travis's side, but it was obvious all was not well between them. His face was set in hard, stony lines and her manner was artificially bright, her eyes cold as green ice.

Whatever had passed between them on their ride was their business. It was Kerry's to see that Davey got his promised game with his father. Davey also was quick to remind his father about it.

Alicia walked away, her head held high and her riding stock flicking her shiny black boots. Kerry wondered whom she wished she had beneath its lash.

Rather unwillingly, Simon sat down beside Davey, who began explaining the game to him. But there was tension in the atmosphere and Kerry moved away, hoping that, alone, they would relax and enjoy their game.

She chatted with a young woman who was watching some horses being rubbed down, but she was near enough to hear what was going on behind her and it was not long before she heard Simon Travis say, 'Let's leave it till another day, son.' Angry and hurt for Davey, she looked round at them, just as Simon put an arm round Davey and drew him close. Davey responded with a quick hug. Kerry turned away again, so as not to intrude on the brief moment of affection between them and, after a minute, was aware that Simon was standing behind her.

'We'll be leaving soon, Sister,' he said. His expression was closed and his eyes remote. Now was not the time to remind him to call her Kerry. He moved off to where Alicia was farewelling other guests, and Kerry began gathering Davey's possessions together.

'We're going home soon, Davey. Could you help me fold the rug, please?'

Davey stood up. He was very quiet. His eyes had the anxious look she had seen in them in hospital and beneath his tracksuit top she saw that his chest heaved slightly. She said, 'I'll go and tell Daddy we're all packed up.'

Simon Travis and Alicia were deep in conversation, standing apart from the other guests. Kerry interrupted them without compunction. Simon looked at her sharply when she asked, 'May I have Davey's aerosol inhaler? I think he needs it.'

He turned quickly and looked at Davey, at the same time feeling in his pockets.

'It's not in the bag?'

'No.'

He clicked his fingers in exasperation. 'I remember—Aunt Thea put it on the table before we left. I must have omitted to pick it up.'

Kerry was appalled. How could a father, who was also a doctor, bring his asthmatic son on a prolonged outing such as this without any medication? She recalled how scornful he had been of her on her first day in her new job, when she had not been able to tell him details of Davey's treatment. That was excusable. This was not.

She said tightly, 'Then I think we'd better leave at once.'

Alicia raised her eyebrows in mock surprise at hearing Dr Travis addressed thus. She laid a hand on his arm, but he shook it off impatiently, and moved across to Davey.

Davey was coughing tightly by now and there were small hollows appearing at the base of his neck with each intake of breath. He was clearly reacting to the tension he had sensed in his father, and Kerry was furious that Simon Travis had not had the sense to hide his feelings about Alicia from his son.

She did not wait to be ushered into the car this time but settled Davey in the back seat and climbed in beside him. Simon started the engine, then turned and looked back at her. 'I think we should go straight to the hospital,' he said.

He was overreacting, as usual. This was a simple attack of asthma which only required simple treatment, which they should have had with them. Kerry had felt Davey stiffen against her arm at the mention of hospital, and said promptly, 'I think home is the best place, don't you, Davey?' Davey nodded gratefully and relaxed against her.

The Mercedes ate up the miles into town. As Kerry talked soothingly to Davey, she began to realise with horror what she had done. She was, after all, only a nurse, and a young one at that. Simon Travis was the town's leading surgeon. Yet she had made it very clear what she thought of him for leaving Davey's inhaler behind. She had practically ordered him to take them home immediately, and then, to cap it all, she had blatently countermanded his suggestion that they take Davey to hospital.

She wanted to get Davey home and treated quickly. For herself, she dreaded the moment of confrontation with his father which she knew must follow.

The Travis home was much as Jo had described it. As

Kerry sat in the car waiting for Simon to take Davey from her, she saw a sprawling bungalow, flanked by modern homes but secluded from its neighbours by a high brushwood fence and a large garden. A wide verandah ran across the front of the house and returned to an entrance halfway down one side. On the other side of the house was a tennis court and, beyond that, Kerry could glimpse the blue of a swimming pool. The house and grounds looked well enough cared for, but they lacked the perfect manicuring of Alicia's.

As Kerry followed Davey and his father into the house, an elderly woman appeared in the hallway, looking anxious. Kerry suspected that the expression was habitual—that the woman spent her days trying to please and her nights worrying about whether she had done so. She was plump, with fair hair faded to insignificance, and a kind face, despite the harried look.

Simon broke in on her anxious flutterings when she saw Davey in his arms. He said reassuringly, 'Don't worry, Aunt. There's no cause for alarm. David just needs his inhaler.' He stood Davey on the floor beside him, and belatedly remembered Kerry.

'Aunt, this is Sister Kerry Martyn. My Aunt Thea,' to Kerry.

Aunt Thea said, 'How do you do?' distractedly, and moved to take Davey under her wing. But his father interposed.

'We'll leave David to Sister Martyn, Aunt. She's been managing him very well so far.' Was there veiled sarcasm in the remark?

Aunt Thea looked downcast at being thus passed over, but brightened when Simon said, 'Sister would probably appreciate a cup of coffee after she's settled David down,' and she trotted happily off to the kitchen.

Kerry followed Davey to his room, where he demonstrated that he could use his inhaler unaided. Before long, his breathing improved and his coughing quietened. Kerry sat by his bed until his eyes became heavy, then she dropped a kiss on his head and crept out of the room.

The clink of cups led her to the sitting room. It was a large, long room with mellow, deep red carpet, some beautiful pieces of old furniture and many of what Kerry guessed were 'Lori's lovely things' that Jo had mentioned, throughout the room.

In a huge bay window at the far end of the room was a coffee table and easy chairs. Simon Travis turned from looking out of the window and watched her as she walked towards him. To the question in his eyes, she replied, 'He's fine—all settled down for a nap. After all that fresh air and excitement he'll probably sleep the night through.'

She took the chair he indicated and he seated himself with his back to the window, his face in shadow. He was watching her, and she wished that she too could hide her face in shadow, away from that probing glance.

She turned to Aunt Thea, and they warmed to one another as they drank their coffee and chatted. Aunt Thea was a dear, ingenuous soul, clearly fond of Davey although finding him something of a worry. Simon she patently adored. In fact, thought Kerry, she had yet to meet one person who did not either respect or adore Simon Travis. Why could she not share their sentiments?

Simon said little, perhaps brooding over what had taken place between himself and Alicia Holmes. Or deciding what to say to Kerry when they were alone, about her presumptuous behaviour at the picnic?

Too soon, Aunt Thea rose and gathered up the cups, murmuring that she must see to dinner. She glanced at her nephew, silently asking whether Kerry would be staying, but he said, 'I shall be driving Sister Martyn back to the hospital shortly, Aunt. I may check up on one or two patients while I'm there. David should be all right. If you need me, you can ring the hospital.'

Kerry stood up as Aunt Thea departed. Simon rose too, and they stood facing one another, with only two or three feet between them. She wished he was not so disturbingly close. She could not move back because of the chair behind her.

She decided not to wait for Nemesis to catch up with her, but to take the initiative. She would apologise, but she would not eat humble pie. She might have treated the town's leading surgeon as though he were a medical student, but she had done it out of concern for his son. Her voice was firm and confident as she said, 'I owe you an apology, Dr Travis.'

'Oh?' he said absentmindedly. Though his eyes were on her face, she knew he had not heard a word she had said. Clearly, Alicia still occupied his mind to the exclusion of everything else, thought Kerry, exasperated, yet at the same time relieved that there seemed no point in pursuing the conversation further.

She moved slightly, intending to pick up her handbag which was lying on the corner of the coffee table. Before she could do so, his arms, as hard as steel, were around her, and his mouth was on hers, forcing her head back.

She was so completely taken by surprise that for several stunned moments she could not move, could not think. Just one word drummed in her mind. Alicia. Alicia.

Simon's arms now were moving down her back, forcing her body against his, and his mouth had left hers and was seeking the hollow at the base of her throat. In a flash of self-revelation, she knew that she was experiencing no emotional reaction at all, apart from stunned amazement that this should be happening. Then, illogically, she thought, it's not happening to me— it's happening to Alicia. I just happen to be here.

She raised her hands, planted them firmly on his chest and pushed him away. He stepped back and, without looking at him, she picked up her bag and said in a quiet, cool voice, 'Will you please take me home.' Then, turning away, she walked towards the door.

Simon spoke from behind her—an apology of some sort, but she was still feeling so detached, as though this was all happening to someone else, that she could not afterwards recall the words he said.

An onlooker would have seen nothing amiss as he opened the car door for her, walked around and took his place behind the wheel. All Kerry hoped was that this sense of detachment would last until they reached the hospital. So, as soon as he had reversed out of the driveway and they were on the road back to the hospital, she said, in a normal, conversational tone of voice, 'I hope Davey is all right now. I'm sure it was just a transient attack.'

Simon's tone was as normal as her own as he replied, 'I agree.' Then he continued, 'You seem to have succeeded with David in a very short space of time, whereas I've failed for years. I wonder what your secret is?'

It was a relief to escape into such a safe, neutral subject.

'I don't have a secret,' Kerry said slowly. 'I have no idea why Davey has accepted me as he has, but I would like to use the confidence he has in me to help him, if I can.'

Even as she spoke, she realised that here and now she had an opportunity that might not come again. She said, 'I think one of his problems is that he so desperately needs to know that he's important to you—more important than all the other things that demand your attention.'

He nodded. 'I *am* busy—perhaps too busy. But David is very important to me. He always has been.' He stopped abruptly, perhaps recalling the six months when he had deserted Davey while he nursed his grief over Lori.

'They say his asthma is some sort of emotional reaction towards me,' he continued.

'So I heard,' Kerry responded carefully.

'Then how does a father deal with that situation?' Suddenly his voice was harsh, tortured, demanding an answer that she could not give.

'He needs a mother . . . Aunt Thea . . . you can see for yourself . . .' Simon threw up one hand.

'I can see she's a dear and that she loves Davey, but I agree, she's not the ideal person to have so much responsibility for a small boy. On the other hand, you could do worse.'

Simon looked at her, sharply, questioningly. She was thinking of Alicia and she knew he was too. He expelled his breath through his teeth, abruptly, in a sigh of pure frustration. Unexpectedly, Kerry felt a deep sympathy for him. She could not understand his attitude towards herself. She had no idea what the situation was between him and Alicia. But she could understand his sense of failure and futility about Davey.

The short drive to the hospital was over and the car was pulling up in front of the Nurses' Home.

Simon turned and looked at her and she knew he was really seeing her this time. His eyes were kind and his voice was very gentle as, laying one hand over hers as it rested on her knee, he said, 'Thank you, Kerry . . . for Davey and . . . for everything.'

Thank you for ignoring that scene in the sitting room—they were the words he was not saying. What he did not know was how different was her reaction now. What his forcefulness had not done earlier, his mere touch and the kindness in his voice accomplished now, and she was devastated by her response. She knew she had to say goodbye and leave without him suspecting the tumult that was raging within her. If she did not, they would never be able to behave with any semblance of normality towards one another again.

Her face was hidden from him as she bent to retrieve her handbag from the floor of the car. She managed to say in a reasonably normal tone, 'Goodbye and thank you,' as she opened the door. Then she was out of the car and walking on legs that threatened to give way beneath her, towards the door of the Home.

She reached her room, caught a glimpse of her burning cheeks in the mirror and covered them with her hands. She went to the hand-bowl in the corner of the room and splashed cold water on her face. Patting it dry with a towel, she dropped into the armchair and took deep, slow breaths until her emotional turmoil subsided somewhat. She had to ignore, she could not allow herself to think about, the implications of her response to Simon Travis's touch.

Action! That was what she needed now. Reaching for her lipstick and her comb, she reassured herself, as she used them, that her tell-tale flush had subsided, then made her way to the kitchen, whence came a babble of voices and the some aroma of coffee.

Most of the morning staff, now off duty, seemed to be gathered there. Every face turned in Kerry's direction as she entered and all lit up with interest when they saw who it was. Several voices spoke at once.

'Hullo. Back so soon?'

'How was your date?'

'Did you have a good day?'

Kerry laughed. 'Spare me, and I'll give you a full report, though there's not much to tell. We went to Alicia Holmes's place for a barbecue and had a lovely day—most of it, anyway. I met a lot of friendly people who all knew Davey and made a great fuss of him. It was too much for him in the end, though. He started an attack of asthma and we had to get him home in a hurry.'

She saw a gleam of added interest on Jo's face and went on quickly, 'We got Davey settled down, had a cup of tea with Dr Travis's aunt, and then he drove me home. And that's it! Except that I've been sitting around all day and am desperate for some exercise. Does anyone feel like a game of tennis before tea?'

'Not me, I'm beat.' 'I'm dead on my feet,' a couple of voices said. Jo said, 'Good idea. Vicki and Sue are always keen to play. I'll see whether they're free.'

'Great! I'll slip into a tracksuit and see you in five minutes.'

The tennis court was behind the Nurses' Home, shielded by it from the windows of the hospital. Vicki and Sue both played well. Jo lacked a little in style but was a firm, strong hitter, and Kerry was able to thoroughly and satisfyingly pound the ball, as though she were driving out of her mind thoughts that had no business there. In fact, the competition became so keen that she forgot everything else as she gave every ounce of her concentration and skill to the game.

When it was over they all collapsed, laughing and exhausted, on the grass beside the court.

'You're good, Kerry. Where did you learn to play like that?' Sue asked.

'Yes,' said Jo, 'you look as though a puff of wind would blow you away, but there's strength in those puny muscles.'

'Actually, I surprised myself,' said Kerry. 'It must have been the competition. It really was a good game.'

'We'll have to do it again some time.'

Chatting casually, they made their way back to the Home for showers and tea.

Jo, naturally, was not satisfied with Kerry's condensed version of her day's outing, but there was no opportunity to discuss it at more length until after tea, and by then Kerry felt she could handle it without her feelings betraying her. Jo, of all people, must not suspect any change in her relationship with Dr Travis, if, indeed, change there was.

'Well?' said Jo, when they were alone. 'Aren't you going to fill me in? What did you do all day? Do you feel any different about Simon, after spending a day with him?'

'To be accurate, I spent the day with Davey. I was fascinated to meet Alicia Holmes, after what you'd told me of her. She was everything you said—treated me as though I were ten years old—all but gave me a lollipop.' Jo nodded, with understanding. 'And neither she nor Dr Travis thought it necessary to introduce me to anyone.'

'How appalling! You must have had a ghastly day!'

'Not at all. We got on very well without their introductions. Your Mount Myall people are so warm and friendly. I can't wait to see more of them.'

'Hmmm.' Jo's eyes were searching Kerry's face. 'I'm starting to run out of leading questions, so I'll ask you straight out. Why the aura of suppressed excitement—whatever it is that made you play tennis like one possessed?'

'Now you're being psychic again!' laughed Kerry.

'I wish I were. You're hiding something, my girl.'

'Not really. There *were* some rather tense moments. Alicia and Dr Travis had a fight. No—not in public—while they were riding. They were all but spitting at one another when they came back. That's what caused Davey's asthma. And his father had left his aerosol inhaler at home, and I told him what I thought of him and ordered him round as if he were a first-year nurse. Then, for good measure, I added a few suggestions about how he could be a better father.'

Kerry burst into laughter at the stunned expression on Jo's face. 'So you see,' she continued, 'I've done absolutely nothing to endear myself to your Simon. I'm just going to have to live with the consequences, I guess.'

CHAPTER SIX

THERE WERE no consequences.

Simon Travis too must have resolved that their relationship be on a strict doctor/nurse basis. His only patient in the Children's Ward was Terry, and when Kerry met him there his visits were brief and his attitude punctiliously professional. At least there was no return to his old hostility.

Then Terry went home and for two weeks Kerry did not see Simon at all. Time passed slowly. She knew there was a vacuum in each long day but did not dare ask herself what it was. She told herself she must be bored. And never before in her nursing experience had she been bored.

Her date with Peter was the one bright spot in an otherwise tedious period.

Peter had asked her to leave the arranging of the evening entirely to him. All she knew was that it would include dinner and a movie and that he would call for her at six-thirty.

There were only two cinemas in town. One was showing a third-rate movie and the other *The Man from Snowy River*. She guessed this would be Peter's choice. She had seen it in Sydney but would be quite happy to do so again. Mount Myall people, with their love of horses, would probably flock to see it. Simon might be there—her heart lifted. With Alicia—the lift subsided.

Peter arrived punctually and nodded approval of Kerry's outfit—slim white pants with a lilac top, a bulky white necklet and matching earrings.

As they did not have long to eat, she expected Peter to take her to a small café or a quick-food restaurant. Instead, he turned away from the centre of the town and eventually stopped the red Porsche in a new suburban area. Kerry, puzzled, looked around for a restaurant, then turned to Peter.

'Where . . .?'

He raised a humorous eyebrow and swept an arm in the direction of a block of modern units.

'Chez Treloar! The best cuisine in town.'

'And the chef?'

'Pierre! *Ooh, là là! Superbe*!'

Kerry had to laugh, though hoping that Peter did not have anything in mind other than a quick pre-cinema meal. He saw her momentary doubt and hastened to reassure her.

'It's a genuine invitation to sample my filet Mignon—not to view my etchings.'

'Promise?'

'Scout's honour!'

Peter parked the car expertly in its allotted space and opened the door to his unit with a flourish. They entered a large, very modern sitting room. Beyond a divider screen, Kerry could see a small round table set for dinner for two, with shining glass and silverware and candles waiting to be lit.

Peter, clearly enjoying himself, watched her look around.

'Pierre needs a hand in the kitchen. Would you like a drink before dinner?'

'Later, thanks.'

'Then make yourself at home, *mam'selle.* Dinner will be served stat'—with a sudden descent from sophistication to the medical terminology which was second nature to them both.

He disappeared and Kerry sat down in a cream leather armchair, sighing rapturously at its comfort. She looked round her curiously. So this was Peter—modern, immaculate, comfortable. Several shelves of books, a hi-fi, a television set with a video cassette recorder, two or three good pictures on the walls. Obviously, he was not such a Philistine as he had made himself out to be. And if he could cook too . . .

He could. Prawn cocktails in a delicious sauce and cupped in crisp lettuce leaves were followed by filet Mignon, as he had promised, and a green side salad. Fresh strawberries in cut-crystal comports, and a bowl of cream, rounded off the meal.

Kerry sighed luxuriously. 'That was superb. I really must go to the kitchen and congratulate Pierre. Perhaps I can help him with the dishes?'

'No need. He absolutely insisted on having a dishwasher.'

Kerry helped Peter carry the few remaining dishes through to the kitchen and stood watching as he loaded them into the washer. Then she looked at her watch. She had not wanted to hurry the meal, Peter had put so much thought into its preparation. But already they would have missed the beginning of the movie.

Peter had yet another surprise in store for her.

'I thought we'd have coffee while we watched the movie.'

He walked into the sitting room, took a video cassette from the top of the bookcase and slipped it into the machine on top of the television set.

'Well,' said Kerry, 'this evening is full of surprises.'

'So long as you're enjoying it.'

'I really am. This is much more congenial for a tired nurse than a cafeteria and a cinema.'

'I thought it might be. I couldn't consult with you

about the choice of a movie without letting the cat out of the bag. I hope you approve. It's *The Verdict*, with Paul Newman. Have you seen it?'

'No, but I've heard it's very good.'

'Then I'll put the coffee on. The bedrooms are upstairs, incidentally.'

'Thanks.'

Upstairs, Kerry found one large and one smaller bedroom, a dressing room and through it a large, modern bathroom.

For a young doctor, Peter had clearly done well, thought Kerry, looking around her, to own a Porsche and a unit like this. Or did he have independent means?

When she went back down, they settled themselves on a long settee, drank their coffee and chatted—shop talk, mostly. It was very congenial, very relaxed. When Peter pressed the remote control button to start the film, it was the most natural thing in the world for Kerry to slip off her shoes and swing her feet up on to the settee.

As they became absorbed in the movie, it needed just a touch from Peter's hand for her to lean back against him. She could feel his breath on her hair and once she thought he dropped a kiss on it. But it was so light she could have imagined it, and it would have been silly to react or even appear to notice. At some stage Peter's arm crept around her waist, but, when his hand moved higher and cupped her breast, she sat up, reached for the remote control panel and pressed the pause button.

She looked at him quizzically. 'You promised!'

'I know. I'm sorry! It won't happen again.'

He looked so penitent she could not help smiling and, emboldened, he added, 'But you're a very tempting lass.'

'Let's keep it cool, Peter. It's early days yet. It's nice to feel so comfortable with you. I'd hate to spoil it.'

'Friends, then?'

'I'd like that.'

The rest of the evening passed easily, and when Peter drove her home and they were standing beside the Porsche it did not seem at all beyond the bounds of the friendship they had agreed upon for Kerry to reach up and kiss him lightly on the cheek.

'Thanks, Peter. It's been an unexpected evening, but a lovely one. It was good of you to think of doing all that.'

He was looking at her wistfully.

'Moonlight becomes you, Kerry. You're sure . . .?'

'Quite sure,' she said hastily. 'Goodnight, Peter.'

She ran lightly up the steps of the home, then turned and waved as Peter reluctantly got back into his car.

Kerry was thoughtful as she prepared for bed. She hoped Peter was not going to be a problem. She had thought he understood that she had no intention of becoming involved in anything but a very casual relationship. She knew what she meant by a casual relationship—someone to talk to, an occasional relaxed date such as they had had tonight—but did it mean the same thing to Peter?

It was not just that she planned to major heavily on her work for some time to come. It was that, at this stage at least, her feelings for Peter were no more than friendly. She had not really minded him touching her tonight. But there had been no response, no fire, nothing like . . .

She turned hastily from thoughts that clamoured.

After all, Peter was so comfortable to be with. Perhaps, in time . . .

Next day, when Kerry came off duty, she found she had had a mystery phone call. The caller had not left her name but said she would ring again later. Kerry supposed it was the mother of one of her patients, wanting to speak to her privately, as sometimes happened. When the call came it was Aunt Thea, and she sounded even more harassed than she had when Kerry had met her previously.

'Miss Milner! What a nice surprise! I hope Davey is all right?'

'Oh, yes, he's quite well. And please call me Aunt Thea—everybody does.'

'I'd love to. And you call me Kerry.'

Kerry waited for Aunt Thea to continue. Then it all came out in a flood.

'Davey has been asking for you, Sister—Kerry. I haven't known what to do about it. Simon has been so difficult and—and cross—I can't imagine why, and I didn't want to upset him any more by telling him about Davey. He's been fretting—Davey, I mean, not Simon. He really does want to see you, but I didn't want to bother you.'

'I'd be happy to see him, Aunt Thea, but only if his father gives his permission.'

'Oh, I *am* glad! Thank you so much. Davey will . . .'

'But, Aunt Thea,' Kerry interrupted firmly, 'I said I could only see Davey if his father consented.'

'Oh, but he has!' Aunt Thea chirped. 'I plucked up courage and asked him. He wasn't very happy about it, but he said as long as he wasn't bothered about it and didn't have to see you . . . Oh, dear! I shouldn't have said that. I'm sure he just meant that he was too busy.'

I'll bet he did, thought Kerry grimly. Aunt Thea's voice was trembling as if she were on the verge of tears. In recent weeks Kerry had begun to hope that Simon Travis was not the egotistical, self-opinionated man she had first thought him. But if he could reduce to such a state his kindly old aunt who had given up her own life to care for him and his son, then clearly her first impressions of him had been accurate. And he had said he didn't want to see her! Well, neither did she want to see him, and she would take good care that they did not meet or she might be tempted to say something to him she would regret.

Aunt Thea was still twittering away on the other end of the line, seeming unconscious of Kerry's long silence.

'Aunt Thea,' Kerry interrupted her again, 'I'm sure we can arrange it that I can see Davey without bothering Dr Travis. I have my own car. I could pick Davey up after school one day and take him to a playground for an hour or so and then bring him home. That way, I wouldn't be likely to see Dr Travis.'

'That *would* be good. Simon sees patients at his rooms every afternoon till about five o'clock. Thank you so much. I can't say . . .' She was almost incoherent with gratitude.

Poor old soul, thought Kerry. She's probably been agonising over this for days, before plucking up courage to take things into her own hands, and now she can't believe she has succeeded. Once again, Kerry gently stemmed the flow of Aunt Thea's thanks and arranged a time and place to meet Davey, after school, two days hence, when she was on morning duty.

All went as planned. Davey was in Junior Primary and finished school at two-thirty. Kerry had time to change out of uniform, meet him and spend an hour in the park with him before returning to the house, well within what she regarded as her curfew of five o'clock. She even had time to chat with Aunt Thea, who was still worried about her nephew's relapse into moodiness and bad temper.

'I thought he was getting over things,' she said. 'He was so much happier for a while, almost normal, but lately . . .'

'Perhaps I can explain that,' said Kerry. 'I don't know whether I should mention it or not, but it may set your mind at rest if I do. On the day of the picnic, Dr Travis and Alicia Holmes apparently had a quarrel. I have no idea what it was about, but he was very upset when they came back from riding. I'm sure Davey was aware of it and that's what brought on his attack of asthma. It could account for Dr Travis's unhappiness since then, too.'

'Alicia Holmes! I'm not surprised.' Aunt Thea's darkened features showed she had no more love for Alicia than had Kerry or Jo. 'But no,' she went on thoughtfully, 'that doesn't explain it, after all. You see, it began before then. I know, because Simon was like a bear with a sore head all the week *before* the picnic.'

Don't I know it! thought Kerry. A week before the picnic would take them back to the day she had seen him on the road. She could not believe that small incident had so upset him as to affect his family life. It was more likely that that day also he and Alicia had quarrelled. Alicia had looked far from happy then, too.

Aunt Thea was saying, 'You know, Kerry, I really thought he was getting over . . . things . . . Do you know about . . .?' Aunt Thea habitually left her sentences unfinished, and Kerry filled in for her now. 'Yes, I do know about Lori. What a tragedy it must have been for you all!'

'They were so happy. Everyone said what a perfect couple they were. Actually, you know, I never met Lori. My home was in Perth and I really do hate aeroplanes, so I didn't come to their wedding. And then Lori was gone.'

Simon Travis would not want her discussing this part of his life with Aunt Thea, so, although she could understand Aunt Thea's desire to share her problems, with a sympathetic listener, she guided her on to another subject, and before long said goodbye and left.

The second time she picked Davey up from school was uneventful also. Kerry stayed a little longer this time, accepting Aunt Thea's invitation to a cup of tea, in the large modern blue-tiled kitchen where everything was spotless and gleaming. Davey had gone off, with a glass of milk and a Vegemite sandwich, to watch *Sesame Street.* Aunt Thea looked round her with justifiable pride.

'I've loved this house from the time I came here. And Simon has bought me everything possible to make things easier for me. He's such a kind, thoughtful man. If only . . .'

Kerry quickly reverted to the subject of the house.

'It may seem odd. I'm a stranger, but I love this house, too. It has such a warm, lived-in feeling. It feels as if it's occupied by lots of friendly ghosts who've loved it in the past and want everyone to love it now.'

'Ghosts?' Aunt Thea did not look too happy at the idea of ghosts in her lovely home. Kerry laughed and patted her arm.

'Don't worry! Maybe I feel like that about the house because you've been so kind to me, Aunt Thea. And Davey too.' She refrained from adding, 'And in spite of what the owner of the house feels about me.'

The third time she had arranged to pick up Davey, it rained. Kerry rang Aunt Thea to say she would collect him from school and bring him straight home. She felt secure now, knowing that Simon always consulted until late in the afternoon.

Davey had learned a new song at school and asked Kerry to sing it with him. She sat down at the upright grand piano in the sitting-room and accompanied herself and Davey. She had not heard him sing before. He obviously had a musical heritage from someone, with an extraordinary ability to remember a tune, and a clear, true voice about which he was quite unselfconscious. Kerry modified her own soprano to his and they sang together the haunting melody.

'There's a lake in South Australia,
Little lake with lovely name.
And the story woven round it

From the piccaninnies came.

Carrabarra Wirracanna . . .'

So engrossed were they that neither heard the front door open and quiet footsteps approach the sitting room. Kerry had no idea how long Simon had been standing in the doorway, listening, before Davey stopped singing and said, 'Hullo, Daddy.'

Kerry whirled round on the piano stool. Standing up and reaching for her handbag from the top of the piano, she prepared to leave immediately, saying, in confusion for which she hated herself but which she could not control, 'I'm sorry—it rained! It must be later than I thought. I must go. I'll see you another day, Davey.'

She put her arm briefly round Davey's shoulders and moved towards the door. But Simon was standing in the doorway and made no move to let her pass. He was looking at her and his face was set, his eyes dark and inscrutable. She was furious that she could not prevent the flush she felt mounting her cheeks. Furious, too, that she should be made to feel like a guilty schoolchild, when she had been giving up her time to amuse this man's son. If Simon Travis had not failed in his responsibilities as a father, she need not have been here at all.

She blurted, 'You're home early.' In her discomfiture, it sounded like an accusation and not, as she had intended, an explanation of why he had found her in his home, against his expressed wishes.

He raised a sardonic eyebrow. 'It *is* my home,' he pointed out sarcastically.

The last shreds of Kerry's brittle composure broke.

'Yes, and Davey *is* your son, and if you spared a little more of your time and attention for him you'd realise that he needs children of his own age for company. In case you haven't noticed, I *am* a few years older than he is. Or aren't the children around here good enough to play with Dr Travis's son?'

As soon as she stopped talking she was aghast at herself and waited for the thunderbolt to fall. But, again, he took the wind out of her sails, leaving her feeling absurdly deflated and slightly ridiculous. As though he had not heard a word of her diatribe, he remarked, with a half-smile, 'You have a lovely voice, Sister.'

A lovely voice! Which she had been using like a fishwife!

Although he spoke to her, his eyes were on Davey, and she knew, to her further humiliation, what he was doing. He was defusing the situation for Davey's benefit. Davey had been standing, watching, only partially understanding what was going on. Aunt Thea had appeared in the passage behind Simon, looking distraught at the sound of Kerry's raised voice, but she seemed reassured by Simon's calmness. Kerry spoke to her, ignoring Simon's remark about her voice, and following, with an effort, his example of establishing normality.

'I'm going now, Aunt Thea. I hope you have a good morning at bridge tomorrow. 'Bye, Davey.'

All she could manage for Dr Travis was a stiff inclination of the head in his direction, and then she moved, again, to pass through the door. He stood aside for her and followed her into the halfway, opening the front door for her. As she went through it, he said quietly, 'I do appreciate what you're doing for David, Kerry.'

Her throat contracted and hot tears suddenly burned behind her eyes. She nodded, not trusting herself to speak. She could have handled sarcasm; again, it was his kindness that unnerved her. She walked the short distance to her car, without looking around, and drove out of the gate and into the street.

It was early yet. Kerry did not want to return to the

hospital until she had managed to regain some measure of control over her feelings, so she drove through the outskirts of the town, till she was out of sight of any human habitation, and there she stopped the car. It was a secluded and peaceful spot on a side road, and she wound down the window to let the cool breeze fan her cheeks. The faintly pungent smell of the bush wafted in and there was the ever-present background of birdsong which was so much a part of the native setting that one really only became aware of it if one stopped and listened for it. Just now, Kerry's senses all seemed heightened, her thoughts tumbling chaotically over one another.

She reviewed the scene she had just left, and, to her mortification, realised that there had been no scene except that which she herself had made. Simon had not said a word out of place. He had merely looked at her and she had flown at him like some little gamecock, thirsting for a fight. And she had done it in Davey's presence, after condemning his father for not shielding him from just such tensions. It was his finding her in his house after he had said he did not want to see her there that had sparked her tirade. But, try as she might, she could not rationalise her behaviour to the point where she could forgive herself for it. How could she ever face any of them again? She wished she had never come to Mount Myall. Nothing like this had ever happened to her in Sydney, but Simon Travis would be the last person to believe that. If she had wanted to confirm his initial impression of her as being too young, too immature, for a responsible position, she could not have gone about it more successfully.

She had tea in a little café in town and returned to the Nurses' Home in the early dusk. Her equanimity was somewhat restored, though still very fragile.

Feeling that company would be preferable to more solitude, she went to the sitting room and found several

Sisters, in various stages of exhaustion and relaxation, idly talking shop. They greeted her with cries of welcome.

'Where *have* you been, Martyn? We thought you were lost.'

'Jo even rang Dr Travis's house, but they said you'd left there ages ago.'

Kerry was bemused. 'I went driving after I left Davey, and then I had tea in town. But why did you need to find me?'

'Matron wanted to see you, but when you weren't back by five, she said we could tell you instead.'

'Tell me what?'

'That you're being transferred to Casualty.'

'But I've almost another week to do in Kids!'

'Kids has been slack and they're short in Cas, so you're to start there tomorrow afternoon.'

'That's great! I love Cas.'

The Sisters looked at on another, assuming expressions of mock horror.

'She loves Casualty!'

'Poor thing! How shall we tell her?'

'Better not tell her. Let her find out for herself.'

Exasperated, but laughing, Kerry threatened them. 'If you don't tell me here and now what you're talking about, I'll . . . I'll . . .'

'Perhaps we should tell her in the morning, so she can have a good night's sleep first. She'll need it.'

'You sadistic wretches! I implore you—tell me, stat.'

'OK. Now hear this.' It was the Sister in charge of Men's Surgery, Monica Barrett, who spoke now. She was a thin, middle-aged woman with a brusque manner and a dry wit. She took a long draw on her cigarette, and continued.

'You may have enjoyed Casualty in your old hospital, my dear, but Cas in Mount Myall is like Cas in no other hospital. It's been Matron's biggest headache since it was set up as a separate department when the hospital was modernised a couple of years ago.'

'But why should it be? Everything else about the hospital is absolutely top-notch.'

'It's not the equipment. There's plenty of that. The main problem stems from trying to run a casualty department without resident medicos. The doctors, who of course all live in town or nearby, originally agreed to be rostered to staff Cas. But they resent like hell being dragged away from their televisions, or their game of golf or their evening meal or what-have-you, when they're called, and more often than not you're left holding the can, keeping some poor accident victim on ice or soothing agitated relatives until a doctor belatedly appears.'

Another Sister broke in. 'We have OP clinics, of course, but emergencies don't seem to understand that they should happen between the hours of eight and twelve.'

'And that's not all of it,' Sister Barrett continued. 'Every doctor has his own pet ideas or preferences about everything—procedures, drugs, whatever. We have lists all over the place about who likes what, but you can't cover every contingency, even if you had time to read the lists when there's a flap on.'

'It sounds like chaos unlimited. But can't Matron or Sister in charge do something about it?'

'Every new Sister who comes along starts off all bright-eyed and bushy-tailed, with brilliant new ideas, and changes things. Then she finds out she still can't get the doctors to co-operate. So she too gets discouraged and gives up. Matron has said that she's not interested in any more band-aid therapy for Cas, and she won't allow any more half-baked schemes to be tried, until she's sure she's got the Sister who can handle it. We're beginning to think her super-Sister doesn't exist.'

'So what you're all really doing now, in your own funny little way, is warn me not to try and change the status quo, but muddle along too.'

'She catches on quick, this girl.'

'We're telling you for your own good, my dear, so you won't be discouraged. If you feel a bright idea coming on, squash it. Just make the best of things as they are, and don't blame yourself if they're not as good as you would like them to be.'

'And is there anything else I should know before I venture into this bear garden? What kind of cases do you get?'

'Fairly typical. Lots of VAs, of course. What Cas doesn't? There's a bad stretch of road on the highway about twenty miles out. It's perfectly straight for miles and the speed maniacs can't resist it. A lot of interstate transports use the highway, and they push up the statistics too.' Lori, thought Kerry.

'And there's a big timber mill, over the hills, northwards.'

'Yes. Suturing's our speciality.'

'And a paper-processing mill sends in its quota of trauma victims.'

'And football teams . . .'

'And swimming pools . . .'

'And careless mothers with adventurous children . . .'

'And battered wives . . .'

'Enough! Enough! I surrender.' Kerry threw up her hands. 'I solemnly promise I'll lie awake all night and will approach my time in Cas with a due sense of grim foreboding.'

She went to bed with plenty to think about, but not unduly worried about what she had heard. Certainly it would be different from what she had been used to. Sister

Casualty, back in Sydney, had been there for as long as anyone could remember, and she ruled her domain with a benevolent rod of iron. But she always had medicos on tap who knew what was expected of them and who accepted the regimen because it had been tried and proved good over many years.

A premise of another kind began to form in Kerry's mind, but she put it from her. After today's débâcle at the Travis home, she had no reason whatever to feel the least bit elated about the fact that she would certainly see more of the hospital's doctors in Casualty than she had in Kids.

CHAPTER SEVEN

CASUALTY was beatifically peaceful, the cubicles empty, polished and gleaming, when Kerry arrived there the next day. But she knew how quickly things could change from calm to chaos, and she was glad to take advantage of the lull to go through the Unit, noting the contents of cupboards, checking stock and drug supplies, trays, instruments, batteries. And trying to memorise the lists of doctors' preferences—*that* would take some time.

For two days, outside of regular clinic hours, they had only a trickle of minor cases which did not cause more than a ripple on the surface calm but did serve to show her how the system worked and also the capabilities of her two nurses. Helen McCusker, the senior girl, was brilliant, alert and responsible. Sadie Bruce, the junior, lacked Helen's experience, but she was keen to learn and to put into practice what they were being taught in lectures.

On the third afternoon, Kerry sat down with the two girls and discussed, in detail, what would be required of each of them, including herself, as members of a trauma team in some fairly typical situations. The next day she staged a mock cardiac arrest and, after a little more drilling, felt reasonably satisfied that they could all work together smoothly, when the need arose, as it would sooner or later.

It arose that evening. At seven-thirty the buzzer rang. Two ambulances were on their way in with victims of a two-car collision. The driver of one of the cars, a nineteen-year-old youth, had gone through the windscreen, probably not wearing a seat belt, and was in the first ambulance.

'There are no obvious signs of bleeding,' the officer said, 'apart from superficial abrasions, but his skin is cold and clammy. Systolic pressure is palpable at 60, respiratory rate is 42 and he's tachycardic at 140. Estimated time of arrival is fifteen minutes.' The second ambulance would arrive a few minutes later, with the occupants of the other car, a middle-aged couple. They had remained inside their car and their injuries were superficial—shock, contusions, possible concussion or whiplash.

Kerry replaced the phone, feeling her senses respond and sharpen. This was nursing. She had spent too many weeks at ease in the Children's Ward and was more than ready for a challenge, her first is Casualty.

Before dialling a number on the internal system, she knocked on the glass of the duty room enclosure and beckoned in the two nurses, who were filling stock drums at a bench. They stood beside her, listening, as she relayed to the nursing supervisor the report she had just received from the ambulance officer. This saved her having to repeat it for the nurses, and, at a nod from her, they went off, to begin preparing cubicles for the admissions. The nursing supervisor would call the doctors who would make up the trauma team, but first she asked Kerry whether she felt she could handle it without extra staff. Kerry said she was confident she could—she had two excellent nurses—but if she found she needed more staff she would certainly request it. Would Sister also, please, alert the X-ray technician and the laboratory Sister? Sister promised to do so, and Kerry hung up. So far, so good.

Kerry joined Sadie Bruce and nodded for her to continue what she was doing as she talked to her. She would need to prepare two cubicles, for the two older patients, who seemed to have minor injuries only. 'Sister,' she said, 'is calling one doctor to attend to them, and I would like you to assist him, please. If you find that their injuries are more extensive than we think, or if you run into problems of any kind, you're to contact Supervisory Sister immediately and she'll arrange more assistance. She'll also see the parents of the injured boy, so notify her when they arrive.'

'Yes, Sister.'

Kerry went to where Helen McCusker was working. 'Nurse, you and I will assist the doctor with the badly injured patient. We should have ten minutes before he arrives. Let's get on with it.'

It was a busy ten minutes. They had to be ready for any contingency. The ambulance officer had not reported fractures or bleeding, but they could not rule them out. The patient would certainly be shocked and concussed. He could have internal organ damage, spinal cord injury, brain damage, lacerations . . . They hung up bottles of intravenous fluid, prepared phials to receive blood specimens for grouping and matching. While Nurse checked that the necessary equipment was to hand for cutting away the patient's clothing and cleaning him up, Kerry opened a suture tray and a cut-down tray, adding antiseptic lotions and preparing a syringe with local anaesthetic.

By the time the ambulance arrived, everything that could be done in advance had been done.

The patient's name was Kevin and he looked too young to have been driving a car. His hair was plastered damply on his forehead, black against the pallor of his skin as he lay unconscious on the table. The X-ray technician went into action immediately, taking his first batch of films, then moving his machine into a corner, to be used again later.

Kerry checked Kevin's vital signs and assessed his coma score. She was not happy about his breathing and suspected lung damage. She hoped that the doctor who had been called would not take his time about coming.

She was listening, intently, through her stethoscope, to Kevin's blood pressure, which was barely palpable, and did not look up when she heard swift footsteps through the Unit. She was aware of two figures donning caps and masks, and of a nurse assisting them with their gowns. Two doctors, thought Kerry thankfully. They could certainly use two doctors for this patient.

As one of them moved into her range of vision, her mind went blank for a second, as though a slate had been wiped clean. She had not considered the possibility of Simon Travis being called. He gave no sign that he recognised her but moved immediately to Kevin's side, raising a questioning eyebrow at Kerry, who, in a steady voice, immediately gave him the information she had gleaned about Kevin's vital signs.

It flashed through her mind that this was the first real opportunity she had had to prove to Dr Travis that she was a nurse worthy of his respect. Then every thought other than that relating to the patient on the table was wiped out.

The other doctor, having scrubbed briefly at the bowl in the corner of the cubicle, moved in to intubate the patient. He caught Kerry's eye and winked. Peter! She was glad that Peter was here. Then the team moved into action.

There are doctors who talk incessantly in operating theatre or emergency room, but Simon Travis was not one of them. But, although he said little, there was no lack of communication and every member of the team knew exactly what he was finding and what was required of them. His eye was keen, his mind quick and decisive and his long hands deft and sure, as he observed, probed, interpreted diagnostic signs, gave his orders, repaired Kevin's damaged body.

Kerry had always loved being a member of a smoothly functioning surgical team, wholly concerned with the problems of its patient and bringing all its expertise and learning to his aid. Tonight her senses were unusually sharpened, so that she seemed to see, from outside, even as she worked, the form on the table, the bright light focused on him, the green-clad, intent figures surrounding him, to hear the beep-beep of the cardiac monitor and her own quiet voice reporting the vital signs the doctors needed to know, as they worked.

As Kerry had suspected, Kevin had lung damage, one lobe of his left lung being collapsed. It took somewhat longer to confirm that there was a slow internal haemorrhage which required surgical repair. It was another hour of concentrated effort before Simon stood upright, flexed his shoulders wearily and said, 'He'll do for now. He can be transferred to theatre for pre-op. See to the pre-med, Peter, please.'

Though they had not said so, Kerry knew that both doctors would stay on to perform the surgery, and, when the trolley taking Kevin to the theatre had squeaked away down the corridor, she despatched Helen McCusker to see to the business of providing coffee for them.

As she removed her mask she said to Simon, 'Kevin's mother is in the waiting room. Sister Cowell will have spoken to her, but would you care to see her too? And then there'll be coffee in my office.' He nodded, looking at her in a way he had several times before and which she always found hard to interpret. It was as though he was coming back from somewhere a long way off, was slightly startled to see her, and could not quite remember, for the moment, who she was.

But she didn't have time now to stand pondering the whys and wherefores of Dr Travis's behaviour. She found Sadie Bruce happily polishing the chrome legs of a table in one of the cubicles that had been used for her two patients.

'All well, Nurse?'

'Yes, thanks, Sister. Dr Anderson had some suturing to do on Mrs Bellis's arm, but that was about all. Mrs Bellis was rather overwrought, so when Doctor was sure there was no concussion, he ordered sedation and admitted her for overnight observation. Mr Bellis is staying in too. How's your patient, Sister?'

'He's stable enough now for surgery. He has a small duodenal tear which the doctors are going to repair. I must report to Sister and get back to them. I'll fill you in later.'

Kerry returned to her office. The two doctors were sprawled in easy chairs, provided for just such occasions. Simon Travis's legs were stretched out, his fingertips were together and his hands covered his face, so that she could not see his expression. She did not disturb him. He was probably thinking about the surgery he would shortly be performing. Peter was his usual animated self and was eager to talk, to make up for the enforced constraint he had had to observe during the past few hours. Kerry knew it would not have been easy for him. After all, he was a specialist in his own right, but, knowing his veneration for Simon Travis, she was not surprised that he bowed to his wishes and worked in silence.

Peter had taken his cap off. His auburn hair was damp and flattened where the cap had been, but, round his face, it had curled itself into ringlets so that he looked like a red-haired, green-eyed cheeky cherub.

He said to her, 'I didn't know you were in Cas, Kerry. When did that happen? You didn't mention it at the movie the other night.'

'I didn't know then. It was rather sprung on me. But I'm thrilled. I've always loved working in Casualty.'

'It shows. You do it well. You have the makings of a good Casualty Sister.'

Simon opened his eyes and flicked a glance in their direction, but, if he had been going to make any comment, it was forestalled by the arrival of Nurse Bruce with a tray, laden with coffee pot and cups, a large plate of freshly made ham sandwiches and a bowl of crisp green salad.

'Nurse, you're a scavenger after my own heart,' said Peter. 'You must give me some tips on how to rustle up a feast like this in the middle of the night. We were just saying what a great job you and Sister did tonight. Congratulations.'

Nurse Bruce blushed furiously, said, 'Thank you, Doctor,' and scurried out.

Kerry laughed. 'So that's how the famous Treloar charm operates! It *was* nice of you to say that, Peter, because she did do well tonight. And Cas staff, if what I've been told is true, need all the encouragement they can get.' She poured coffee and handed the two men their cups, placing the tray of food where they could help themselves.

Peter said, 'Ah, the perennial problems of Casualty—of which we doctors, it seems, are chief. But greater men than I have beaten their brains out trying to solve them, so let's not talk about them now. What *is* important, in view of your shift to Casualty, is whether you still have Saturday night off for the Ball. I'll break my heart if I have to sit home alone, lamenting.'

'I'm sure Nurse McCusker would love to save you from that fate worse than death. If it was necessary—but it's not. I've been given my same days off.'

There was no flicker of interest now from Dr Travis as he sat, coffee cup in one hand, a sandwich in the other, his eyelids almost closed. He probably, like many doctors, could snatch a catnap any time, thought Kerry, to help them survive the demands of schedules like this. How different the two doctors were, yet they each obviously respected the other, and they worked admirably together.

Excitement mounted during the week preceding the Ball.

There had been no elective surgery booked for that week, so that as many of the staff as possible could go to the Ball. In the Home, on the night itself, excitement rose to fever pitch, with everyone showering, titivating, popping in and out of rooms, seeking advice, reassurance, a helping hand.

Kerry's dress was of palest gold chiffon over taffeta, with shoestring straps. Its close-fitting, swathed bodice showed her shapely bust and tiny waist off to perfection. The skirt was full and ankle-length. She wore bronze high-heeled strappy sandals and a light-as-air scarf round her shoulders. She had drawn her hair high on her head and tied it so that it fell in a gleaming cascade at the back. The style accentuated the delicate bone formation of her face, the finely traced eyebrows and large grey eyes. Her skin glowed with health, country air, youthful vitality and what was left of her Sydney tan.

Peter's look, when he called for her, was eloquent.

'I'm going to be the envy of every man at the Ball tonight. I'm sorry I don't have a golden carriage to transport you there, but my humble chariot awaits.'

Kerry grinned at him. 'Knowing what you think of your humble chariot, the honour is all mine,' she said.

Peter glanced sideways at her several times as he drove into town. 'Lady, if you dance like you look, I'm going to have one enchanted evening.'

Kerry smiled. Peter being Peter, she was not too overcome by the fulsomeness of his admiration. 'You do realise that the staff are supposed to socialise as much as possible, Peter, rather than stay exclusively with their own partners?'

'Yes. I promise I'll do my duty, as long as you reserve every other dance for me.'

'Perhaps we'd better wait till we've danced together. We might find we tread all over one another. I hope you don't mind,' she went on, 'I've arranged that we form a party with Jo, Vicki, Sue and their partners. Vicki is married and only lives in the Home when duty demands it. She has two very nice brothers who are partnering Jo and Sue tonight. I haven't met them yet, but, if they're as much fun as Vicki, they'll do.'

It *was* fun, from the moment they entered the huge, decorated hall and their party of eight gathered, with much lighthearted jollity. They had tables at the edge of the dance floor. Kerry soon realised that Peter would be more at home in a disco than at a formal dance, but what his dancing lacked in finesse he made up in enthusiasm, and he was so popular with both staff and townsfolk that their tables became the centre of merry, chattering groups, between dances.

Kerry was more acutely aware than she wanted to be of Simon, tall and very handsome in a dinner suit. He was with Alicia, of course, a stunningly beautiful Alicia in a violet faille dress with halter neckline, her blonde hair in sophisticated swirls atop her poised, elegant head and long neck.

Alicia was playing, with gracious perfection, her role as a member of the hospital Board, and Kerry thought that one could assess one's social rating by the effusiveness of Alicia's greeting. Kerry rated a brief nod. Peter, wickedly tongue-in-cheek, was held in animated conversation for several minutes and, as the music began again while they were still talking, he felt it was his bounden duty, so he told Kerry later, to ask Alicia to dance.

Simon was standing not far away, as Peter and Alicia joined the dancers moving on to the floor. He glanced in Kerry's direction, and her heart stood still. She knew, in a flash of self-knowledge, that it was for Simon, and not for Peter, that she had wanted to look her best tonight. Feeling slightly suffocated, and in control of neither her breathing nor her heartbeat, she hoped and yet feared that he was about to ask her to dance. She was not looking directly at him, but she knew that he was moving towards her and she took a firm grip on her composure.

'Good evening, Sister.'

'Kerry,' she reminded him, her grey eyes twinkling.

'May I have this dance, Kerry?'

'Yes.'

It meant nothing, of course, him asking her to dance. All the doctors had been dancing with nurses and Sisters, as well as with their own partners and friends. But as she went into his arms Kerry knew that, for her, this was a very special dance.

He danced divinely, his arm firm and strong about her, leading her through the intricate steps so that she felt as light as thistledown and gave herself up to the sheer joy of it. She was glad he did not talk and did not appear to notice her silence. She wished only that the music might go on for ever, that she never had to leave the circle of his arm, that she could lay her head on his breast and be comforted, as she had seen Davey do. Which was quite irrational, because the only things she needed comforting for were the problems he himself had caused her. But love is not rational, and the knowledge burned in her, so that it could no longer be ignored—she loved Simon Travis.

When the music stopped, they drew apart and stood,

not clapping as the other dancers were, but looking at one another. Kerry dared not speak. She did not know what she could possibly say, nor how her voice would sound if she tried to use it. Simon put a hand under her elbow and they moved towards the table where Jo and her partner were already sitting. He said, 'Thank you very much,' and moved away.

Peter claimed her immediately for the next dance, and she was thankful. Jo would have seen at once that everything was not as it had been before. The glow inside her gradually surfaced, but she was not aware that she looked at Peter with radiance in her face. She did not know that Peter, seeing the glow and believing it to be for him, thought, Wow! and then, Am I ready for this? and raised a little barrier of caution.

She was not aware, either, that Simon, dancing by with Alicia, also saw the glow and, thinking it was for Peter, went through the motions of the dance mechanically, while his mind slowly firmed into a decision.

Later in the evening, Simon danced with Kerry again. They danced together almost as well as they had before, but this time the magic was not there. Kerry, on her guard against her own treacherous heart, began talking lightly as soon as the music began, and he fell in with her mood. He was not, now, the reticent man she had known. He was charming, talkative, and quite impersonal. Above the music of the band, they exchanged chit-chat about the weather, the hospital, Davey. Several times their dancing took them near where Alicia was sitting out the dance with a partner. Her smile was a mask, set and artificial, and she stabbed angrily at an ashtray with her cigarette.

A few moments later Jo danced by in Peter's arms, and, seeing her face, Kerry knew, in a swift, illuminating flash, that Jo, in Peter's arms, was experiencing what she herself had, earlier, in Simon Travis's arms.

Jo and Peter!

How blind she had been! She had jumped to the conclusion it was Simon for whom Jo was carrying a candle. She recalled prattling on to Jo about Peter having asked her to the Ball. No wonder Jo had been unnaturally quiet and unresponsive that night!

But Peter had told Kerry he was a free man—that his affections were not engaged. So what were Jo's chances? About as good as hers with Simon! Kerry resolved on the spot to do all in her power to make things work out for Jo. Thank goodness her own feelings were not engaged with Peter. She must make that quite clear to him, and to Jo.

Simon had felt Kerry stiffen in his arms. He saw her eyes on Jo and Peter and he put his own interpretation on why she had suddenly become quiet, seeming not to have heard his last remark. He too fell silent, and they finished the dance, each occupied with their own thoughts.

Kerry contrived not to dance again with Peter, and when it was time to go home she suggested brightly that their group meet for coffee back in the Sisters' lounge. On the way home she parried Peter's suggestion that they stop for a while, and when they arrived home she got out of the car immediately, avoiding his reaching arm. She said warmly, 'Thank you so much for taking me, Peter. Its been lovely,' and kissed him impersonally on the cheek, before leading him inside.

She made sure that when they said goodnight later on it was in the presence of them all, including Jo, so that Jo could see that there was nothing between herself and Peter.

Peter went home, to ponder on the fickleness of women, who beamed on a fellow as if he was the light of their life one minute, and cold-shouldered him the next.

It had been a night of revelation for Kerry and she pummelled her pillow for hours, trying to woo sleep and turn her thoughts off Simon Travis. But they would not be turned off. She lived and relived those moments in his arms, not denying, now, what was in her heart. She was as sure that she loved him as she was that he had not the slightest feeling for her, beyond, maybe, gratitude for what she had done for Davey. That, without a doubt, was why he had invited her to dance with him. He had been repaying an obligation with a courteous social gesture.

More than ever, she must place a guard on her emotions and never, never allow him to glimpse what was in her heart.

'Cool professionalism. Cool professionalism.'

She went to sleep repeating it, hoping that her subconscious mind would get the message and not play her false in the future.

CHAPTER EIGHT

In the following week, Casualty went mad. Emergencies snowballed into an avalanche, and before long Kerry was only too aware of the frustrations she had been warned she would encounter working in the Unit, even with the extra staff Matron sent to help.

As Junior Casualty Sister, Kerry was still working mostly the afternoon and evening shifts, but relieving Sister Casualty on morning duty on Sister's days off.

Sister Casualty was a local girl, Benita Allen, who had recently married. Not having known her previously, Kerry was not able to assess whether the lack of enthusiasm she showed for her job was consequent upon her marriage, or whether she had gradually become disheartened because of the problems within the Unit. Or whether, in fact, Matron had put her there as a stopgap, knowing that she was not likely to make changes in the organisation of the Unit.

Matron's wishes notwithstanding, Kerry felt that certain changes, even if they were only temporary, would help them through this hectic period without causing too much wear and tear on the nerves of doctors, patients and nurses. She made one or two tentative suggestions, and when Benita accepted them without resentment, though not evincing much interest either, felt justified in taking the reins a little more firmly into her own hands.

Matron, who always knew just what was happening in her hospital, took to dropping in at unscheduled times, as well as during her regular daily round of the whole hospital.

Simon, too, began to appear at odd times. He would sometimes wander in after he had finished in theatre, help himself to coffee from the café bar and relax in one of the easy chairs in the office. Kerry wondered whether this was his usual practice, and felt a little disconcerted at first. But he did not seem particularly interested in what was going on in the Unit and gradually Kerry, although never unaware of his presence, found that she could go about her duties much as she usually did.

He was in the office one day when she walked in to call a doctor for a patient who had just presented, following an accident at a sawmill. She smiled a brief hello at Simon then, with one hand on the telephone, stood consulting the list of doctors, wondering whom to call.

'Can I help, Sister?'

She turned at the sound of the quiet voice from the chair.

'Would you? It's a lacerated foot—a clean laceration. It shouldn't take too long.'

'Then let me know when you're set up and Nurse has thoroughly cleaned the foot.'

Normally, Kerry would have assigned one of the nurses to assist with a routine job like this, but, as Simon had volunteered his services, she felt she herself should assist him.

As usual, he did not speak much as he worked and, as Kerry had predicted, he completed the suturing in less than half an hour. Standing on the side of the table, watching his long fingers skilfully injecting local anaesthetic, then wielding the holder with the curved needle and fine silk thread, Kerry felt—not disturbed as she feared she might, but a deep sense of contentment, or satisfaction . . . she would not allow herself to analyse her feelings further.

On the next occasion she had to call a doctor when

Simon was in the Unit, she approached him tentatively.

'Would you mind . . .?'

'Not at all.'

And so it happened several times, and each time she assisted, and each time there was that strangely peaceful aura. He seemed to have completely buried whatever hatchet it was he had been wielding earlier, and Kerry began to understand why Jo and Peter and everyone else praised him so highly.

Off duty, she put what little energy she had left after her hectic day's work into plotting how to bring Jo and Peter together. Peter had been called to Casualty several times and was his old carefree self, friendly as always, clearly accepting the casual nature of their relationship.

At the end of the week, something happened that put even Jo and Peter out of Kerry's mind.

Late on Saturday morning, as she was checking that the reports on the morning's cases had been properly completed, the phone rang.

'Sister Martyn? Simon Travis.'

'Yes, Dr Travis?' His tone was formal and she assumed that he was calling about a patient.

'Tomorrow is your day off, I believe. Would you care to have lunch with us? At our home, of course.'

Her heart thumped hard for a moment. It was the first time she had been invited to a meal at the Travis home, and though Davey had probably initiated the invitation Simon had said 'with us', so presumably he intended to be there.

Carefully she replied, 'It *is* sometime since I've seen Davey. Tell him I've missed him and would love to come.'

'Aunt Thea said one o'clock. Is that convenient?'

'Yes.'

'We'll see you at one, then.'

The next day was warm and Kerry dressed for the visit in a slim, pale blue, sleeveless linen frock. Simon himself opened the door to her, but he had barely had time to greet her when Davey rushed through the hall and launched himself into her arms. Misty-eyed for a moment, Kerry hugged him tightly.

Aunt Thea's welcome was more restrained but no less sincere. She led them into the sunny dining-room, its table set with flowers and dainty crockery. The lunch she had prepared was light and delicious—a seafood mousse with salads followed by a strawberry pavlova.

Davey could not wait to tell Kerry that Aunt Thea was taking him to play at a friend's place after lunch. Kerry was absurdly disappointed that her visit was to be so brief a one.

Davey's spontaneous chatter was welcome because Simon seemed preoccupied, though cordial and at times even charming. Aunt Thea seemed unusually restrained and twice stopped herself in mid-sentence, with a hand raised to her mouth and a guilty glance in her nephew's direction. Kerry sensed that there was something, a family matter, probably, that Simon wanted kept private, which was causing the constraint. By the end of the meal she was thankful that her visit would soon be over.

After lunch, Kerry helped Aunt Thea carry out the dishes and watched as she loaded them into the dishwasher. Then she stood with Simon at the front of the house, waving goodbye to Davey and Aunt Thea.

Simon chuckled as Aunt Thea's car moved slowly out of the driveway.

'If we ever sell that car,' he said, 'we can truthfully advertise it as having been owned by one little old lady who's never driven it above fifty kilometres an hour.'

'She's a dear. I love her,' said Kerry impulsively.

He turned to look at her. 'The loving heart,' he said,

a trifle sarcastically.

Kerry flushed and retorted, 'Why not? There's enough of the other thing in the world today.'

'You're right. I'm not decrying it—just wondering how far your loving heart would be prepared to go.'

She had no idea what he meant and no desire to pursue the conversation along those lines, so she took her keys from her bag and turned to walk towards her car.

Simon stopped her with a hand on her arm.

'Kerry,' he said quietly, 'would you mind staying a little longer? It was I, not Davey, who wanted to see you today. I have something to ask you.'

She stood, mystified and irresolute.

'Come inside?'

She turned and walked in front of him, back into the house.

Inside, he opened a door on their left and motioned for her to enter a room she had not seen before. It was obviously his study and very much a man's room. Medium sized, it was carpeted in dark blue, patterned with gold. One wall contained a large stone fireplace, with bookshelves set back on either side. The other walls were lined with bookshelves below, and above were panelled with timber, with the lovely patina of age. The panelling set off to perfection three modern Australian paintings, obviously the work of one artist. Kerry liked them but could not identify the artist. Pro Hart? Not quite. There was a large desk, leather-topped, and two deep black leather armchairs. The only other chair was behind the desk. This was a room for tête-à-têtes—and it was evident that was what they were about to have.

Simon motioned her to one armchair and sat down in the other. The distance between them was not great. After a moment he gave her a long, considering look and began slowly:

'We haven't known each other long, Kerry, so I hope you won't think the favour I want to ask of you presumptuous. The fact is, we're in somewhat of a dilemma. Aunt Thea's sister, my Aunt Edith, who lives in Perth, has had a stroke and Aunt Thea is anxious to go to her as soon as possible.

'Edith has her own family in Perth, but the two sisters have always been close and I can understand Aunt Thea's desire to see her now, even though the prognosis is quite hopeful.'

He paused and Kerry said, 'I thought she had something on her mind at lunchtime.'

'Yes. I'd asked her not to mention it until I'd had a chance to talk with you.'

Kerry began to have an inkling of where the conversation was leading, but she waited for him to continue.

'We'll have no problem getting someone in to do the housekeeping while Aunt is away. There's a capable woman, a Mrs Hamilton, who has helped out in the past when Aunt has been away for bridge weekends. We managed very well for those short periods, but I want Aunt Thea to stay at least a month when she goes, and I've been at my wits' end to know what to do about Davey for that time. We have friends who would happily take him, but he's been so much better in the last few weeks that I'm reluctant to risk upsetting things by sending him away from home.'

If Alicia Holmes is the friend you have in mind, thought Kerry, I heartily agree.

'Is this Mrs Hamilton not able to live in?' she asked.

'Oh, yes, she'll be living in. She's excellent at what she does, but she would be no companion for Davey.'

Kerry, by now, was quite sure she knew where the conversation was heading, and was also sure of her response, so she interposed before Simon could go any further.

'I would be happy to come as often as I can to see him while Aunt Thea is away,' she said. 'Perhaps on my days off I can take him on a trip or a picnic . . .'

She was really looking forward to the prospect, she found, and Simon could not but be aware of this. There was warmth in his voice as he replied, 'Aunt Thea was right. She was quite sure you would help. But, actually, we had intended asking a little more of you than that, and you must say if you think it would be too much for you. After all, you're still settling in to your new job.'

Kerry raised questioning eyebrows but allowed him to continue.

'In spite of being so much better, David still has problems. He's been subject to nightmares since . . . his mother died.' The last words were laboured, as if it was an effort for Simon to utter them. 'He has the occasional temper tantrum, which you've never seen. His school tells me he has a high IQ, but he's a slow learner. Yet, with you, he seems eager to learn. Then there's the question of his asthma. He coughs a lot at night and occasionally needs a mask. I can usually take care of this, but I'm often called out at night. You've helped David so much already, we wondered whether you would be prepared to live here for those weeks, be here for him at night and during your off-duty times when you're not otherwise engaged.'

Kerry did not know what to say. This was more than she had expected and she needed time to consider it. It was not that she was unwilling to do it for Davey's sake. And there would be no problem about living out—after all, many of the staff did so. But living in the same house as Simon? Meeting him in all kinds of family and domestic situations—at the breakfast table, in the evenings after Davey was in bed? How fragile was the truce that existed between them at the present time? She was reluctant to do anything that might jeopardise it.

He was giving her time to consider, watching her face, probably reading her indecision in it, but she hoped not the reason for it.

She saw clearly that she could only assess the situation and make a wise decision if she knew the reason for his early animosity towards her.

She said, 'You've put me on a spot. I don't know what to say. I'm as fond of Davey as he is of me and I'd like to help him, any way I can. But,' she took a deep breath, 'you must admit that you and I haven't got along as well as Davey and I have. I've never understood why you seemed so antagonistic to me when I first came here. It would help me decide what to do now, if I knew what you had against me, then.'

A shadow passed across his face and she sensed him withdrawing.

'I'm afraid I can't discuss that. There *were* reasons why I felt as I did, but they were personal ones and you were not in any way to blame. They need not affect your thinking now. I hope we can leave it at that.'

His voice was toneless but very firm, and Kerry knew it would be useless to press him further. But she was more puzzled than ever. At least she knew that his animosity had not been a figment of her imagination. Perhaps living in the house, *en famille*, would throw some light on it. She made up her mind. She would do as he asked, even though she had a premonition she would spend those weeks treading on eggshells.

Before she could speak, Simon said, 'I can see I've put you in a quandary. Would you rather sleep on it and let me know tomorrow?' His voice was kind, concerned for her.

'No, that's not necessary. I'll do as you wish, even though I have some reservations.'

'As far as I'm concerned, you need not.' Kerry read into that a tacit assurance that she need not fear a repetition of his behaviour on her earlier visit.

'Also,' he continued, 'you mustn't feel you have to spend all your off-duty time with David. I don't expect you to put your social life in limbo for a month.'

She smiled. 'I could hardly claim to have a social life here yet.'

Simon raised on dark eyebrow quizzically. 'I rather thought . . . Never mind.'

She knew he was thinking about Peter, but she had no intention of discussing Peter with him, so she said, 'I'll ring Aunt Thea this evening and talk about domestic arrangements, find out when she plans to go, and so on. And I'll speak to Matron about living out for a time.'

'Good. I know one young man who'll be delighted.'

Matron greeted her request with more reservation than Kerry had expected.

'I can see the value of what you propose for Davey. But do you really think it's a good idea for you, personally? People do talk.'

Kerry was nonplussed. 'I see what you mean. But it never ever occurred to me until this moment, and I'm quite sure it hasn't to Dr Travis either, that anyone could misconstrue the situation like that. After all, there'll be a live-in housekeeper. And, although people don't know me very well yet, they do know Dr Travis, and surely his reputation would protect us from gossip.'

'It should. You must do as you think fit, of course. Just remember that Dr Travis is a very eligible widower, and there could be those with their own axe to grind who might not stop at a little mischief-making.'

She's thinking about Alicia, thought Kerry. And she's right. Alicia's nose could well be out of joint that she was not the one asked to help out in Simon's predicament.

Jo had doubts too, and this time Kerry reacted indignantly.

'Jo! You of all people know how little chance there is of any hanky-panky between me and Dr Travis. I'll be there purely as a companion and night-nurse for Davey, and if you think . . .'

'Of course I don't.'

'Then stop worrying about what people might think. It's just not their business. Anyway, if I *were* having it off with Simon Travis, that would be our affair and nobody else's. Surely in these enlightened days . . .?'

'OK, OK! I just don't want you to be hurt. And I'll miss you round the place.'

'Sorry I flared up. I must admit to having mixed feelings about it all myself, and I'll be glad when the month is over.'

Three days later Kerry was installed in the Travis household. She had moved her belongings in that morning and unpacked them in a small but delightful bedroom, on the other side of Davey's room from his father's. Simon was to drive Aunt Thea to Canberra that afternoon so she could take an early morning flight next day for Perth. He had given Kerry a key to the house, saying he might not be back by the time she arrived after evening duty. Mrs Hamilton was already installed and in competent charge of her domain and had been told to ring Kerry at work if there happened to be any problem with Davey in the meantime.

It felt very strange letting herself into the darkened house that night. Simon was not yet back and, as Kerry had had supper at the hospital, she slipped quickly into bed. It was not long before she heard the sounds of his arrival and quiet movements about the house for a time. She smiled, in the darkness, thinking how little she could have anticipated this situation a few short weeks ago.

One evening, towards the end of the first week, Jo rang.

'Hi! Simon's at the hospital for an emergency appendicectomy, so I thought you might be free to chat. Are you?'

'Love to! Davey's asleep and Mrs Hamilton's busy in the kitchen, as usual. I was just thinking how much quieter a house is than the Nurses' Home, and wishing I had someone to talk to.'

'How are you and Simon making out?'

'Would you care to rephrase that?'

Jo laughed. 'Getting along,' she amended.

'Very well—if you can call saying "hello" a couple of times a day "getting along". It's amazing how two people can live in the same house and see so little of one another. And I was visualising long evenings in his company, wondering what we'd talk about!'

'Is he avoiding you, do you think?'

'I don't think so. He may be taking advantage of Davey having a companion to catch up on his reading. There are always medical journals lying about. And he *is* called out quite often.'

'You disappoint me. I was hoping for an exciting rundown on life *chez* Travis.'

Kerry chuckled. 'Oh, there have been one or two hiccoughs.'

'Tell!'

'As long as *you* don't. Matron has warned me to protect my reputation at all costs—not to mention my chastity!'

'I promise. Not a word!'

'On the first night . . .'

Jo sighed rapturously. 'What a delightful way to start a story!'

'Idiot! Any more comments like that and you won't hear the rest of it.'

'I couldn't bear it after that beginning.'

Kerry began again, carefully.

'The first night I was here, Davey had a nightmare. I'd been sound asleep and he was screaming so loudly that I bounded out of bed and made for his room without even grabbing a dressing gown. His father did the same—from the opposite direction—and in the dark we met, very literally, outside Davey's door. I almost lost my balance and grabbed the nearest thing for support—which happened to be Simon.'

Sounds of delighted appreciation were coming from the other end of the phone. 'That must have broken down some inhibitions!'

Kerry continued, 'Mrs H., hearing all the noise, chose that precise moment to appear and switch on the light. And there we were, clutched in each other's arms, I in my shortie nightie, he in his dark blue pyjama pants and a bare manly torso. If Matron had been there, she would have thought her worst fears were realised.'

Jo chortled gleefully. 'And then?'

'We untangled ourselves very promptly. He muttered something like, "Forgot you were here. Carry on, Sister", and fled. I went in to Davey, woke him up thoroughly, quietened him down, went back to bed and to sleep. And that was that.'

'I'm disappointed the end of the story isn't as romantic as its beginning. You could at least say you went to sleep and dreamed about bare manly torsos.'

'Sorry.' Kerry had no intention of telling Jo that a certain bare manly torso had kept intruding itself in her mind's eye at the most unlikely times since that night.

Jo had a further comment. 'Kerry, for the first time I heard you call him Simon. That's progress.'

Kerry laughed. 'That was Mrs Hamilton. At breakfast next morning, we were both being excessively proper and

Mrs H., obviously with the intimate midnight scenario in mind, said bluntly, 'Humph! What's this "Sister", "Doctor" business? You're not in the hospital now!' We both looked coy and embarrassed, but when it was time for me to leave for work, Simon said, "Goodbye, Kerry", and I, greatly daring, said, "Goodbye, Simon". I was grateful to Mrs H. because it would probably never have occurred to him to say, "Call me Simon" and I wasn't looking forward to either being excessively formal or to resorting to something like, "Hey, you!" Well, I've talked enough. Now it's your turn. Fill me in on the hospital gossip I've missed through being here.'

They chatted happily for another ten minutes. During that time Kerry managed to get in a reference to Peter, and the way Jo pounced on it and continued to talk about Peter confirmed to Kerry that she had been correct in assuming that Jo felt something more than friendship for Peter, and also that she no longer regarded Kerry as a rival for Peter's affections.

CHAPTER NINE

THE DAYS were warm and Kerry made full use of the swimming pool in her off-duty hours, an aspect of life at the Travis's that delighted her. Davey enjoyed the water too, and under her coaching his swimming improved markedly.

One warm evening, after dinner, he demanded that Kerry and Simon join him in the pool so that he could show off his swimming prowess to his father. Simon needed very little persuasion. Recalling her conversation with Jo about bare manly torsos, Kerry had to suppress a smile at the sight of him in swimming trunks. It was not so easy to suppress her awareness of his proximity as they swam and frolicked in the water.

Gradually the warmth of the days intensified into a heatwave, and Kerry took to creeping out of bed a half hour earlier than usual for a swim before going to the hospital. The bedrooms were on the other side of the house and she thought she had disturbed no one, but on the second morning, Simon appeared.

Her heart stopped a beat at the sight of him, tall, lean and tanned as he stood on the edge of the pool before diving cleanly into the water. She smiled a welcome and they swam together, up and down, up and down.

It was like that for several mornings. They swam. They talked a little in low tones so as not to waken the others. Then they would meet, cool and refreshed, at the breakfast table.

On Friday morning, Simon was already in the pool when Kerry came through the side door from the house.

She slipped into the water and swam to join him at the far end.

They breast-stroked lazily down the pool and back, then stopped. He said something to her, something inconsequential. She replied and, without warning, his eyes, tense and compelling, were holding hers so that she could not look away. She felt as though she were being drawn into their dark brown depths and lifted on to another planet. Without her volition, their bodies came together. His arms were round her, vice-like, straining her to him. His mouth, wet, hungry, demanding, was seeking hers and she had neither the strength nor the will to resist him.

Her lips parted under his and their kiss was deep and long. Beneath the water his legs were entwining hers. She knew she should be resisting him, but she was powerless to do so, just wanting the ecstasy to continue for ever. Instead, abruptly, Simon thrust her from him, so that a yard of water separated them. His eyes still held hers, but they were angry and hard now as he said thickly, 'I'm sorry,' and turned away.

Desperately, Kerry said to his departing back, 'Simon, don't be sorry! Please, don't be sorry!'

He pulled himself out of the pool as though he had not heard her, picked up his towel and disappeared, without a backward glance.

She stayed in the water a few minutes longer, trying to regain her shattered composure. When she thought Simon would be in his shower, she drew herself slowly out of the water, showered in the poolside change room, crept back to her room and dressed in uniform.

Nobody else was up when she slipped into the kitchen and propped a note against the coffee-pot, saying that she had a busy day ahead of her, had left early and would have something to eat in the Unit.

It was a long day. For brief intervals she was able to lose herself in her work, but her thoughts always returned to those moments in the pool. They were tumultuous, questioning thoughts as she relived the feel of Simon's arms about her, his mouth on hers. What did it mean? Was he beginning to fall in love with her, or was it just a matter of proximity, perhaps of sexual frustration if he had, indeed, been through a long period of celibacy since Lori's death? If it was the dawning of love, then he had rejected it as though it were unwelcome, when he had thrust her from him. There was humiliation at the thought of that rejection.

She felt a different person from the one she had been yesterday. She had thought she loved Simon then. But that had been a pale, anaemic thing compared to this turbulent, chaotic emotion that gripped her now and set her limbs trembling and her mind whirling.

One thing she knew, life in the Travis home for the next few weeks would not be the comfortable, mildly exciting thing it had been settling down to be. Now it would be torment—sweet torment, but torment, nonetheless.

She did not see Simon that day, either at work or at home. She phoned Mrs Hamilton in the afternoon, to say that she would be having tea with Jo, in town, so would not be home to dinner.

It was breakfast time next morning, Saturday, before she and Simon met again. He looked pale but remote, and did not stay long at the table. As he stood up and pushed in his chair he said, curtly, 'I shan't be home today. I'm going riding.'

So his reaction to the incident in the pool yesterday was to go to Alicia. Kerry's heart protested, but there was nothing she had any right to say. She kept her eyes on her plate to hide the hurt in them and did not say goodbye to

Simon as he left.

As usual, Saturday evening in Casualty was busy, a few accident victims, a drunk or two with minor injuries, people with aches and pains. Kerry threw herself into her work, trying not to wonder what Simon and Alicia were doing.

She arrived home at ten-thirty, to find Simon's car in the driveway, lights blazing from several windows and the house in a state of mild turmoil. David had asthma, quite a bad attack, Simon informed her tersely. He seemed to imply that she should have been there, that that was what she was living in the house for. She could sense his relief when she took over. If she had not been due home, Davey would have been taken to hospital, she was sure, and was glad that had not happened.

Davey had had all the medication he was allowed for the time, so she sat by him, supporting him against her and encouraging him to follow her own regular, organised pattern of breathing, to reduce his hyperventilation. When it was safe to do so, she repeated his medication, and this time he improved rapidly and soon became drowsy. She crept away at last and into her own room, without seeing anyone. She lay awake for a long time, wondering whether, in his room down the hall, Simon was lying awake too.

Now began a strange, bitter-sweet time for Kerry. To be living in the same house with Simon, seeing him every day, kept her emotions in a state of constant turmoil. She would not have had it any other way. To have had no other contact with him than his brief comings and goings in the Unit would have been unendurable. It was not as though he said much to her, at home—he almost seemed to go out of his way to avoid seeing her, but there were times when it was inevitable that they spent time in one another's company, if only for meals.

On the third day after the morning in the pool, Kerry received a summons to Matron's office. She still felt tired and drained of energy as she knocked at Matron's door, wondering what the summons meant.

Matron looked at her keenly.

'Are you tired, Sister?' Nothing escaped Matron's eye.

'A little, Matron. David had a bad attack of asthma the night before last and I was up with him until quite late.'

'I'm sorry. I'd heard he was improving. How are you coping with it all?'

'Quite well, really. Apart from the time I spend with Davey there are no demands on me. Mrs Hamilton is very capable and won't let me help with meal preparation or chores. And there are less than two weeks left of my time there.'

'Good,' said Matron, then went on briskly, 'You may not be surprised to learn that Sister Allen has resigned. She finds she can't cope with married life as well as nursing. She will continue working in Casualty for the two weeks until her resignation takes effect, but I want to put someone else in charge of the Unit immediately. I've had good reports from all sources of your work in Casualty, especially during your recent busy period, and I'm asking you whether you would be interested in a permanent position as Sister Casualty.'

Matron raised one hand as Kerry was about to speak.

'I would rather you knew just what the position will entail before you commit yourself. You're fully aware of the problems we've had in the past in running Casualty efficiently. You also probably know that I've been waiting to find a Sister whom I could, with confidence, place in charge there, to institute the changes necessary to make it function as it should. I feel you could be that Sister. I might add that, in offering you the position, I'm acting on a strong recommendation from a senior member of the medical staff.'

Kerry could feel her fatigue slipping away as she listened. This was an opportunity she had coveted but which she had hardly dared hope she would be offered.

'I would very much like to accept the position, Matron. To be honest, I'm excited at the prospect and I already have some ideas I think could be useful.'

Matron said, dryly but with a smile, 'I thought you might have. I would like you to take over immediately. It will mean, of course, that you work the morning shift permanently. Until she leaves, Sister Allen can take the p.m. shift.'

That night, after returning home, Kerry showered and put on a pale blue silk negligee, long and full-skirted. She went to the kitchen, made herself a mug of hot chocolate and was sitting beside the table, sipping it, when Simon walked in. He too was in a robe, a dark brown, short terry towelling one. His legs and feet were bare. He nodded as he went to the refrigerator and poured himself a glass of orange juice. He was about to walk out of the room when Kerry stopped him.

'Do you have a minute, Simon? I have something to tell you.'

'Yes?'

'Matron has asked me whether I'll take over from Benita Allen as Sister Casualty.'

'Oh?'

He did not seem surprised, and a suspicion crossed her mind. 'Matron said that a senior member of the medical staff had recommended me for the position.' Simon said nothing.

'Am I correct in thinking the senior medico was you?'

'Yes, that's so. Have you accepted?'

'Yes, I have. I'm looking forward to it very much. I only hope I can justify your confidence in me—and

Matron's.'

'You'll do well, I'm sure.'

This, it dawned on Kerry, was the accolade she had been determined to win from Simon. But it was an indication of the easing of hostility between them that she felt, not a sense of victory, but of deep satisfaction at having earned his approbation. This, and having been offered the job she had wanted to get her teeth into since hearing of the problems of the Casualty Unit, had made it quite a day.

But it was not over yet.

Simon walked to the sink, rinsed his glass and placed it, inverted, in the draining basket. As he did so, the phone, muted for the night, buzzed in the dining room next door. He walked through, spoke briefly, listened. Kerry heard him say, 'Right away,' and hang up. He returned to the doorway and said, 'I'm wanted at the hospital. It could be a long night.'

In response to her enquiring look, he said briefly, 'An incident with a home-made bomb . . . an estranged, psychotic husband . . . five children, one of them dead . . . the wife critical.'

Kerry was on her feet. 'I'm coming too. I'll be ready when you are.' The night staff would be able to use an extra pair of hands. Saturday nights at the Unit were liable to be busy enough without this sort of emergency.

She dressed quickly, in a fresh uniform. A light was showing beneath Mrs Hamilton's door. Kerry knocked and poked her head in just long enough to tell Mrs Hamilton, who was sitting up in bed with her hair in rollers, reading a paperback, that she and Dr Travis had been called to the hospital and would she keep an ear open for Davey, please.

Then they were on their way.

Briefly, Simon filled her in on what little he knew of the

emergency. The eldest child, a boy of about fifteen, was not home at the time—probably at a disco or movie. The youngest, a two-year-old who slept in the mother's room, had been killed outright. He was not sure of the extent of the injuries of the other three children, but the mother was in a bad way and might not make it. The father was in custody.

They arrived at the hospital just as the ambulance did, its sirens screaming, lights flashing. Simon disappeared into the operating room immediately. Kerry presented herself to the Unit's night Sister, saying merely, 'Where would you like me?' Sister paused long enough to say, 'Great!' and point towards a cubicle into which the first of the stretchers bearing the three children was being manoeuvred. One child was screaming, another moaning quietly, as though only partly under the effects of analgesia.

The next two hours flew by. The Unit was a hive of concentrated but quiet activity. The other patients on the benches sensed the gravity of the situation and waited, subdued and uncomplaining.

By one a.m. Kerry's assignment was finished. The child would live, and without permanent disability. Physical, anyway. Who would say what psychological scars would remain?

Kerry had a quick cup of coffee, debated whether to go home but decided to wait for Simon and took herself off to an annexe where she spent the next hour and a half cleaning instruments and packing bundles for sterilisation.

As she lifted a heavy tray of instruments into the steriliser, she heard Simon's voice in the corridor. Afraid he might not realise she was still in the hospital, she quickly set the thermostat and the timer and went out to him. He looked surprised to see her, and very, very tired.

'Let's go home,' he said, nodded to Night Sister and followed Kerry out into the cold night air.

When they were in the car, she asked, 'How is your patient?'

His voice sounded infinitely weary as he said, 'She didn't make it.'

Nothing more was said during the drive home. It was a silence of shared exhaustion, horror at the tragedy, frustration that as doctors and nurses they could do only so much to save lives and repair broken bodies.

As they entered the house, Kerry said, 'I'll have a quick shower and then make us a snack.' This, she recognised, was what she had waited at the hospital for, the opportunity to minister, somehow, to Simon's need.

Ten minutes later, wearing her blue gown again, she was in the kitchen, filling the electric jug, assembling the makings of sandwiches, when Simon, also in a robe and with his dark hair still damp, came in and silently worked alongside her. Then he carried the loaded tray through into the long, comfortable family room which ran the width of the house at the rear and was furnished with cane furniture and deeply cushioned easy chairs.

He stood while Kerry began pouring tea into cups. She could feel fatigue and reaction to the last few hours beginning to take their toll of her, and suddenly found she could not see what she was doing for blinding tears that filled her eyes and coursed down her cheeks. She straightened and turned towards Simon, meaning to apologise for her weakness.

There was compassion in his dark brown eyes, and understanding. He held out both arms towards her and she walked into them, to be held against his breast as he made comforting sounds while the tears continued to flow.

He reached for a large white handkerchief from the

pocket of his gown and handed it to her, releasing her to enable her to use it.

'I'm sorry!' she said. 'I don't usually do this.'

'I know.'

'It's the children.' Her tears flowed afresh, and again he said, 'I know.' Then, gathering her into his arms as though she were no bigger than Davey, he sat down with her in one of the big easy chairs.

She did not really need the encouragement of his hand to bring her head again to rest on his breast. As his free hand gently stroked her hair, she sensed that he too needed the closeness of these few moments to counteract something of the impact of those traumatic hours at the hospital. Perhaps it was Davey he was thinking of as his voice made soothing murmurings against her hair, wanting to hold and protect him against the kind of tragedy which was becoming so appallingly frequent, to prevent what was his slipping away from him, as his patient had slipped away despite his desperate efforts to save her . . . as Lori had slipped away . . .

Kerry could hear the steady thud, thud of his heart beneath her ear and, as she lay there, the horror of what they had experienced diminished. Her tears had stopped and she felt extraordinarily calm. But she knew she must get out of her present situation and restore some semblance of normality to the scene before awareness and embarrassment set in.

She made a move to sit up, saying, 'I must pour the teas,' as if it was the most ordinary thing in the world for her to be sitting on Simon's knee with his arm around her. But his hand restrained her and both his arms were round her now and his face buried in her hair. He was still being so gentle and undemanding—paternal, she thought—that she did not take fright or offence but was content to lie there until he was ready to release her.

Indeed, she was more than content. She felt deeply happy and peaceful, with no desire to question what all this meant. She just accepted it as an almost inevitable sequel to what they had been through at the hospital.

'You belong here, Kerry,' he murmured, against her hair.

'I'm glad I was here,' she said, and was about to make one more attempt to normalise things by saying that her month would soon be up and she would be returning to the Nurses' Home. But Simon's next remark shattered any pretensions that this was a normal conversation about mundane things.

'Will you marry me?' he asked.

With a single movement, she was off his knee and standing before him, staring at him as though she could not believe what she had heard. He stood too.

'I'm sorry,' he apologised, 'I shouldn't have put that so bluntly. But somehow, everything seemed so . . . right. I thought you felt that too.'

'I did,' Kerry stammered, 'but not . . .' She shook her head helplessly. 'It's too late . . . we're too tired . . . Let's not talk any more now.'

'I won't pursue it now if you'd rather not. But I want you to know that this is not something that's just occurred to me. I've been facing the fact for some time that I'm very reluctant to have you return to the hospital. You seem to belong here with us. I decided days ago to ask you to marry me. I can see it was not the time to mention it. But, as I said, it just seemed to happen in the natural course of things tonight.'

He had not said any of the things she had imagined hearing in a proposal of marriage, but she knew that he was not a man to whom words came easily in an emotional situation and she felt she could read in his eyes, fixed on her face, all that he had not said.

'I felt the same way,' she admitted. Then she heard her voice, almost of its own volition and as though it belonged to someone else, saying, in steady, measured cadence, 'I'm very much inclined to say, "Yes".'

Simon took her hands and held them firmly, looking at her with a kind of wonderment. The wonder became hunger and he took her in his arms and kissed her, deeply and satisfyingly.

Kerry realised that she had been waiting for this moment and her response confirmed what she had known in her heart since the night of the Hospital Ball. When at last he released her, she drew a deep, happy breath and said, 'May I make that a definite "Yes"?'

He hesitated for a fraction of a second before replying.

'I feel I haven't been fair to you. I shouldn't have asked you to make this kind of decision at this time of night. Why not sleep on it and, if you feel differently when you wake up in the morning—or at any time—you must say so.'

Kerry knew she would not change her mind, but, sensing his slight withdrawal and putting it down to fatigue, she nodded and said, 'I promise if I change my mind I'll tell you. Now I shall make some fresh tea and we must catch a few hours' sleep.'

CHAPTER TEN

SURPRISINGLY, and contrary to her expectations, Kerry slept soundly. She awoke at her usual time and heard in the distance the muted sounds of the household at breakfast.

She was reaching for a tracksuit—her usual attire on days off—when she reminded herself that this was the first day of her engagement to Simon, and she dressed instead in a dainty, pale blue casual frock and sandals.

Sleeping on her decision had not changed it, but she wondered how Simon was feeling this morning, whether he regretted having committed himself. She resolved that, until she saw him and could assess his attitude, she would quell her heightening sense of excitement and anticipation and appear as normal as possible.

She need not have worried. He stood up and came to her as soon as she entered the breakfast room. He took both her hands in his, looking down at her tenderly and saying, 'Did you sleep?'

'Yes, very well.'

'Second thoughts this morning?'

'No.'

'Then may we tell them?'

'Certainly.'

'Mrs Hamilton—Davey—Kerry has agreed to marry me!'

They were both delighted, of course. Mrs Hamilton did not seem surprised—she obviously considered it the natural outcome of middle-of-the-night, semi-nude embraces.

Davey was puzzled at first and not quite sure what it all meant, until his father explained to him that Kerry would be living with them permanently after they were married. That met with his unqualified and very vocal approval.

Simon had to go to the hospital to check on patients. He ruffled Davey's hair affectionately, dropped a quick kiss on Kerry's face, upturned to his, said, 'We'll talk later,' and departed.

Kerry spent the hours he was away trying to convince herself that this was really happening. She had a strange feeling she was a character in a play, acting out a part that was already written. She only had to follow the script, which, she felt sure, had a happy ending.

Simon did not confine his activities that morning to his patients. When he returned at lunchtime he brought with him an engagement ring which took Kerry's breath away. It was a white opal, with diamonds, in a very modern setting.

That afternoon, to escape from Davey's happy, incessant questions and Mrs Hamilton's probings about the when, where and how of the wedding, Simon took Kerry to a remote gorge in the hills, through which the river—low, now, in summer—ran, and they talked.

Would six weeks be too soon for the wedding? Kerry gasped but agreed happily.

Should they announce their engagement immediately or allow a little time for the news to leak gradually? Kerry thought that was not necessary. Once they knew of the engagement everyone would be wise before the event. They would have seen it coming—her visits to Davey, the picnic, these weeks spent in Simon's house.

Aunt Thea would be back at the end of another week. Simon would ask Mrs Hamilton to stay on until after the wedding. It would be catered for, but even so . . .

Simon was considerate, tender, affectionate. Kerry

stopped waiting for him to say the magic words, 'I love you', and was happier than she had ever thought possible, though still having an urge to pinch herself to make sure she wasn't dreaming—and to convince herself this was the same man—hostile, remote—that she had known so short a time ago.

The only person Kerry told of the engagement before it was announced was Jo. Jo, remembering Kerry's first impressions of Simon, was reserved at first and put her through a gentle grilling. But Kerry's shining happiness dispelled her doubts and she was unfeignedly glad for them both.

As Kerry had surmised, after the initial stir caused by the announcement of the engagement, nobody seemed very surprised, except, perhaps, Peter and Alicia, who had reasons of their own for their reactions on the news.

Peter came to see Kerry in the Unit. He seemed more puzzled than anything by the news and, as they talked, Kerry realised that it was Simon's role in the affair that surprised him. He obviously expected that any sensible girl would fall for the Boss.

'But I didn't expect *him* to go off the deep end like that, so soon. No reflection on you, old girl. But it does explain why I never felt I was getting to first base with you.'

She twinkled at him. 'I knew from the beginning that the competition was too keen for me.'

'Competition?'

'Your chariot.'

'Oh! You know, there have been times lately when her lines haven't stacked up so well against others I could mention.' Peter looked so forlorn Kerry felt like giving him a comforting hug.

'You and I were meant to be just good friends, Peter. When you *are* ready to fall for someone seriously, don't go too far afield. There could be a gem of fairest ray serene right under your nose.'

'Now what do you mean by that enigmatic observation, I wonder? And, speaking of competition, how did you knock Alicia out of the ring?'

'With the greatest of pleasure.'

'I'll bet!'

He went off, whistling, down the Unit and Kerry thought fondly that some broken hearts are soon mended. Which boded well for her plans for Jo.

Alicia came through Casualty that same day, on her way to a Board meeting and dressed for the part, in a beautifully tailored navy blue suit and snowy, frothy-necked blouse. Kerry was alone in her office and Alicia closed the door as she entered. They could not be overheard, but they could be seen through the glass partition. A visitor like Alicia never went unnoticed in the Unit, and Kerry wondered what interpretation the staff would put upon the visit.

Alicia's green eyes glinted with malice and she vacillated between cold hauteur and barely controlled fury as she talked.

'I suppose you know why Simon is marrying you?'

Kerry was mystified by the question. She was confident she did know why he was marrying her, although he still had not said in so many words that he loved her. She could only reply, 'Yes, I know,' to Alicia.

Alicia was taken aback by the quiet affirmative.

'Have you no pride, allowing him to marry you for such a reason?'

Kerry had no idea what Alicia was talking about, but she was not about to say so.

'Whatever his reason, Miss Holmes, he *is* marrying me, and I know he wouldn't take kindly to any interference with his plans.'

'*His* plans?' The voice was sneering.

'Yes—*his* plans. You'd better believe that, if you want to remain a friend of the Travis family, which I believe is what you call yourself.'

Alicia took herself off in high dudgeon, and Kerry thought hard and long about her visit. It was obvious that Simon had not forewarned her about the pending engagement. But what did she mean about the reason he was marrying her? She puzzled over it, but found no answer and finally decided that Alicia had jumped to some conclusion of her own, or that it was just her way of trying to foment trouble between Kerry and Simon. But the thought of Alicia recurred through the day. She could only guess at what her relationship with Simon had been, or what expectation she had really had of marrying him.

Kerry asked Jo to be her bridesmaid and Simon arranged that they go to Canberra for a day's shopping, flying there with a politician friend of his who had his own Cessna. They spent a hectic and hilarious day.

Kerry chose a delightful old-world bridal gown of cream silk and heavy lace, with a high neckline and long sleeves with wide tight cuffs. It was much too expensive, but the look in Jo's eyes when she tried it on decided Kerry, imagining the same admiration in Simon's eyes when he saw her wearing it.

Jo's dress was next. They finally settled on a light bronzy gold, which had an old-world aura and suited Jo's attractive brunette colouring to perfection. Then they put their heads together over silky underwear, frilly nightgowns and negligees.

In the late afternoon, they piled their purchases into a taxi and were driven to the airport for the flight home. Aunt Thea, recently returned and overjoyed by the news that had awaited her, had invited both girls to dinner, and she listened, rapt, to their account of their day.

Other than Alicia, the only other person who seemed

opposed to the idea of Simon and Kerry marrying was Matron. Kerry thought she knew why—Benita Allen had so recently resigned because she could not cope with the demands of married life and her nursing duties. Kerry went to Matron's office.

Matron greeted her with considerable reserve.

'I should offer you felicitations, Sister, but I must confess to having doubts about your engagement to Dr Travis.'

'I can understand that, Matron, and I've come to assure you that I feel I shall have no problem in handling the position you offered me, as well as preparations for our wedding and, later on, married life. But, as I haven't yet taken over as charge Sister, if you wish to appoint someone else, in the circumstances, I shall understand.'

Matron's eyes were shielded from Kerry as she fidgeted with some papers on the table before her. She seemed patently at a loss, as if there were something she wanted to say but could not find the words. Finally she said, 'How long has this . . . association . . . with Dr Travis been going on, Sister?'

So Matron was upset that Kerry had not mentioned it when she interviewed her about the new job. Kerry hastened to assure her on that score.

'I had no idea, when you offered me the job, Matron, that this was going to happen.'

Matron looked at her sharply. 'Then don't you think you're being a little hasty? Are you really sure this is the right thing for you?'

'Dr Travis and I both feel we're doing the right thing, in spite of having known one another for so short a time.'

'Then nothing I can say will influence you to change you mind?'

'No, Matron.'

'Then I can only wish you well.'

'Thank you, Matron. And the position?'

'The position? Oh yes, the Unit.' She was thoughtful for a moment. 'You know my hopes for the Unit, Sister. It's up to you to decide whether you can give the time and energy to it that it will demand. If so, I'm happy for you to go ahead.'

'I feel I can, Matron, and I would very much like to try. I never intended marriage to interfere with my career, and I'm sure Dr Travis understands this.'

Matron nodded and stood up. The interview at an end, with Kerry feeling that Matron remained unconvinced about the whole situation.

She lost no time in applying herself to the problems of the Unit. Now that Aunt Thea had returned and Kerry was living in the staff quarters again, she was able to put in extra hours on duty as the reorganisation process got under way.

Outside of duty hours, a multiplicity of details and decisions about the wedding demanded her attention. She had hoped that the interval between the engagement being announced and the wedding itself would give Simon and her an opportunity to get to know one another better. But he too was kept busy, and once or twice reacted so irritably when she referred to him matters relating to the wedding that she tried to avoid doing this and make decisions herself, with Aunt Thea's help.

Kerry found herself looking forward to the honeymoon as the opportunity for them to spend the leisurely moments of getting to know one another that she coveted. Then it seemed that the honeymoon, too, would have to be curtailed because of Simon's work commitments and Kerry's responsibilities in the Unit. A long weekend was all that they could hope for, and Canberra seemed to the logical place to spend it. They would be married on Saturday morning of the second week in January, have an informal reception in the Travis garden, then drive to Canberra that afternoon, returning late on Monday.

So when Kerry, looking radiantly beautiful in her lovely dress, exchanged vows with Simon in the old ivy-covered Anglican church in Mount Myall, she almost felt that she was marrying a stranger, that, more than most couples on their wedding day, she and Simon were at the very beginning of their life together, with everything to learn about one another. But she was very much in love and very confident about the years ahead of them.

The local newspaper printed a rather fulsome account of the wedding of the lovely Kerry Martyn to Dr Simon Travis of one of the town's oldest and most esteemed families and an eminent surgeon. One felt the reporters were somewhat disappointed at not being able to describe it as the wedding of the season, but Kerry and Simon had both agreed that it should be kept small and informal.

Most of the forty guests who gathered in the garden of the Travis home for the wedding breakfast following the service were friends of Simon. Kerry's father, and her brother and his wife, Katya, and their three children had motored across from Sydney. Her father was staying in the house, Robert and Katya and the children in a motel in the town.

Kerry had always been close to her father. Her mother had died when Kerry was tiny. She could remember her only as a warm, bright presence and a lovely face in a photograph. Her situation as a child had been very similar to Davey's, she realised for the first time—which could explain her instant sympathy for him. She also realised that she had never seen a photograph of Lori. Perhaps Simon had found it too painful to have them in the house.

She was thrilled to see that her father and Simon had taken to one another immediately and that her father seemed very happy about her marrying Simon, although rather stunned by the suddenness of it.

Once again, looking at the people gathered in the garden, so few of whom she knew, she realised that the past, for Simon and herself, was almost non-existent—everything lay in the future, and she was impatient to take that next step into their future.

Simon was the perfect host, attentive to her family, who knew even fewer of the guests than did Kerry, protective and proud of his lovely bride.

Once or twice Kerry sensed a tenseness in him. But that was understandable. He could not but remember Lori today. Kerry wondered where their wedding had been held. Many of the guests would be remembering Lori too—some might even have been at that first wedding. Kerry would get to know, eventually, which of these people were old friends, which newer acquaintances. Alicia? How far back did she go? Alicia was on her best behaviour today, conscious, perhaps, that people would be watching her, to see how she was taking this marriage of Simon Travis.

Kerry was happy when the time came for her to slip into the house and change into her going away outfit—a slim lemon-yellow sleeveless shift. As Jo helped her, Kerry said casually, 'By the way, Jo, I've asked Peter to see you back to the hospital—duty of the best man, you know!'

Jo, equally casually, but with a slight flush tingeing her cheeks, said, 'Thats fine. Thanks.'

Farewells and good wishes were said, then Simon and Kerry were on their way, in the silver-grey Mercedes.

When they were out of the town but before the road joined the main highway, Simon stopped the car, turned to Kerry, took her in his arms and kissed her.

'That's for my beautiful bride. Happy darling?'

'I couldn't be happier. It was a lovely wedding, if I do say so myself.' She sighed blissfully. 'If only we had a month, instead of a weekend!'

'We will—later on. Right now, we can fit quite a lot into two days.'

Kerry twinkled at him. 'I'm looking forward to it.'

CHAPTER ELEVEN

'ON THE first night . . .'

'What a lovely way to start a story!'

Kerry, lying in bed the next morning, smiled as she recalled that phone conversation with Jo. Then she drew a long, contented breath, wriggled her toes and stretched happily, but carefully so as not to waken Simon who was sleeping quietly beside her.

What a lovely way to start a marriage!

It had been—just perfect! She turned her head and gazed adoringly at her husband, her eyes lingering on the strong line of his jaw, his mouth—firm, even in sleep—his crisp wavy brown hair.

My husband—wonderful word! And this was just the beginning of all the wonderful years ahead of them.

Simon had seemed to enjoy their lovemaking last night as much as she had. If she could go on making him happy—if she could help wipe out the memory of past tragedy. Not wipe out the memory of Lori—she would never want to do that. She did not feel in the least jealous of Lori. Simon had loved Lori deeply—it was not right that he should ever forget her.

Poor Lori. Poor Simon. If their married life had been anything like last night, no wonder he had been shattered by her death.

She reached out a hand and laid it, very gently, on his hair, barely touching it but feeling the need to express, even though he was not aware of it, her understanding about Lori, her resolve to help heal the wounds, her love for him.

Gentle though her touch had been, he stirred and opened his eyes, then turned his head to look at her—a long, considering look.

'Happy?'

'Utterly! I've been lying here, thinking. About last night. About us. And about . . . Lori.'

Simon moved his head on the pillow, abruptly.

'Kerry, you know I got up last night—afterwards.'

'Yes, but I was so sleepy I didn't hear you come back to bed.'

'As a matter of face, I got dressed and went out, walking—walking and thinking.'

'Yes?' She was looking at him, trust and adoration shining in her eyes.

He turned away, as though he did not want to be distracted from what he had to say.

'I walked for quite a long time.'

'What were you thinking about?'

'A long pause. 'About our future.'

'I know we've got a lot to discuss, but do we have to do it now?'

She moved towards him and, after a moment's hesitation, he took her in his arms and laid her head on his chest.

'You're right,' he said. 'We can talk another time.'

There was relief in his voice and she felt him relax as he gathered her closer to him.

They spent the day exploring Canberra, driving through the Embassy area, lunching on the shores of Lake Burley Griffin in the sunshine as a steady stream of lunchtime joggers passed by, viewing the magnificent panarama from the top of Black Mountain.

And they talked—mainly about the past, learning all the things they did not know about each other. Although Simon had said they must discuss the future, he seemed reluctant now to do so, and Kerry found that in all their conversations there were sensitive areas that were better left untouched, particularly any mention of Lori, which revealed to Kerry that those wounds were still deep and unhealed.

That night they made love again, but, as had happened the second time they danced at the Ball, the magic was lacking this time. Simon was unresponsive and Kerry wondered, afterwards, whether they would have made love at all that night if she had not initiated it. She was not too perturbed. It would take time for them to grow together.

Next morning they booked out of their motel, then spent almost two hours in the National Gallery—a blissful time for Kerry, highlighted by her seeing for the first time Jackson Pollock's *Blue Poles.* Simon seemed to derive as much entertainment from seeing Kerry's reactions as from the works of art themselves.

They ate lunch in the Gallery restaurant and then set out on their journey home, driving slowly because the storm which had been threatening all day had broken and heavy rain pelted against the windscreen while lightning flashed in the distance.

They travelled in silence for a while. The heaviness of the sultry weather seemed to be weighing down on their spirits. Kerry wondered whether Simon too was pondering the changes that their marriage would bring to his lifestyle. She wished he looked happier about it.

After a time he broke the silence, saying abruptly, 'I spoke to Aunt Thea on the phone this morning before we left the motel.'

Kerry was surprised that he had not mentioned the fact earlier, but said lightly, 'Oh? How are she and Davey?'

'Davey is well, and excited about our coming back. Aunt admitted to still being tired following the wedding.'

He was silent and Kerry, stealing a glance sideways at him as he drove, was surprised at the tautness about his mouth and the sombre look in his eyes as they watched the road. Had he learned something during that phone call that he had not told her?

Before she could ask whether that was so, he said, 'I rang to ask Aunt to arrange something for me. I explained to her that because I'm so often called out at night, and you have to be on duty so early in the morning, I felt it would be better if you and I sleep in separate rooms. She'll have made the necessary adjustments by the time we arrive home.'

There was a finality about the words and the tone of voice in which they were uttered that precluded discussion of the matter. Kerry understood that she was to accept the *fait accompli* without comment.

She turned her head away from him, looking through the window at the rain-drenched landscape so that he would not see the hurt in her eyes. However sensibile it might be for them to sleep in separate rooms, they were still in the first week of their married life, and who wanted to be sensible then? It was a time for romance, for putting up with some slight inconvenience for the sake of closeness and building a strong basis for their marriage.

And Simon had made the arrangement without consulting her! That was highhanded of him, and insensitive and quite unforgivable. She knew she should tell him immediately how hurt she was by his action, but she could not do so and, analysing the reason for this, she had to admit that she was fearful of his reaction. In fact, she had a sickening, sinking feeling that they were regressing to the state of affairs that had existed between them for the first week or two after they first met.

But that was not possible. She knew Simon now. She knew that he was not the superficial, egotistical man she had then taken him to be. She knew, now, that he could be kind, compassionate, loving, tender.

Colour flared in her cheeks as she remembered how loving, how tender he had been in those moments of shared intimacy the night before last. Nothing could take that away from her. And there would be more times like that, even if they did sleep in separate rooms. Nothing must jeopardise that. She shivered to think how nearly she had come in the last few minutes to laying the foundation of a barrier of resentment and bitterness between them.

Impulsively, she turned to him and said, 'If that's how you want it, Simon.' Then she quickly changed the subject. 'I'm looking forward so much to getting back home.'

The tightness left his face. He smiled at her and replied, 'I am too,' then added, 'You're a sweet child, Kerry.'

Kerry was not sure she wanted to be designated a sweet child by her husband of two days, but, she thought philosophically, it would do to be going on with.

They were given a rapturous welcome home by Davey and Aunt Thea. Aunt Thea had prepared a delicious light meal and over it everyone exchanged titbits of news as though they had been apart for a month.

Kerry left Simon to see Davey settled into bed and read him his story, while she and Aunt Thea cleared the table and talked some more. It became clear to Kerry that Aunt Thea was deferring to her in household matters. She said, 'We should have talked about this before the wedding, Aunt Thea, but there was so little time. Even if I were not working, I couldn't manage the house nearly as competently as you do. It will be a great relief to Simon and me it you carry on as you've always done.'

Aunt Thea glowed with pride at Kerry's praise, and with relief that she would be able to continue to care for the family and house that had become her own.

They all opted for an early night. There was a finality about Simon's brief goodnight kiss at the door of her room that told Kerry she would not be seeing him again that night.

As she undressed in the room she had always occupied, knowing that he was preparing for bed in the room next door, she admitted that he was probably wise—it *had* been a long day—she had to be on duty at seven the next morning and he probably had a heavy schedule to face. But it was still disappointing.

In the weeks that followed, her disappointment grew into a deep sense of rejection, of hurt bewilderment, as night after night she waited for some word or sign or knock on her door.

When none had come by the end of the week, she put on her prettiest negligee and knocked on his door. He opened the door to her, allowed her to come in and closed it behind her. He was still fully clothed and gave no indication that he had any idea why she had come to his room. They talked a little and a short time later Kerry found herself back in her own room, frustrated and furious with the whole ludicrous situation.

When her emotions had subsided somewhat, she told herself that she was too inexperienced at this seduction business. Then she admitted that she was, also, too afraid of Simon's reaction had she pressed her advances too far. She did not want him to put into so many words his rejection of her.

She threw herself into her work at the Unit, working out her frustration in a frenzy of planning, reorganisation, talking to her nurses, talking to doctors. At least Matron was happy with her. And she had, she felt confident, managed to camouflage her feelings so that nobody would have suspected that she was anything but a happy bride in the first flush of married life.

Simon was sometimes rather quiet, sometimes appeared abstracted but, on the whole, was pleasant enough to live with. Kerry examined the situation exhaustively, from all angles, and could make no sense out of it all. She clung to the memory of that first night when he had been so happy and relaxed.

She went back over what they had done, what they had said, that might have brought about the change. Perhaps she should not have mentioned Lori on the morning after —she had sensed some withdrawing on Simon's part then.

For the first time, Kerry felt bitterness towards the memory of Lori. Lori had not been relegated to a separate room, she felt sure. Lori had shared that big bed in Simon's big room, had hung her clothes in the huge wardrobes that lined one side of the room. Her cosmetics had stood on his dressing table. They had had cosy, intimate chats as they prepared for bed in the same room, as they lay in the dark in the same bed . . .

Kerry cut short her imaginings, which were only causing her more anguish. She had accepted that Simon had loved his first wife deeply. She realised that he still had some degree of grief and guilt over Lori's death.

If only he would talk to her about it! She must be patient until the time came that he felt he could do so. In the meantime, she must not do or say anything that would permanently damage their relationship. She must keep everything running as smoothly and normally as possible.

With this in mind, she said, one Saturday morning when she was off duty and they were all having a leisurely breakfast,

'Do you think we should do some entertaining, Simon? People will expect it of us soon.'

He looked up from his newspaper. 'Will they? What did you have in mind?'

'Perhaps a pool party, while the weather is still warm. We could have lunch on the patio.'

A pool party would include Davey. He added his plea, 'Please, Daddy!' Aunt Thea, too, looked pleased at the idea.

'Whom would you ask?' Simon asked Kerry.

'On my side, Jo. And Peter, of course,' Simon looked at her sharply and she added, 'They *were* our wedding attendants.'

'Of course.'

'Then possibly Vicki and her husband. And Sue. We could ask Mark, for company for Davey.' Davey clearly approved. 'And you could make a list of those you wanted to invite.'

Simon considered. 'Why not?'

When he handed his list to Kerry, later, it had Alicia's name at the top, but he had coupled it with that of her manager, Cornish Langton. Kerry rang to invite Peter and added, as if it were an afterthought, 'Jo has been having some trouble with her car, Peter. Would you mind bringing her with you?'

'Not at all.'

When Jo said yes, she'd be delighted to come, Kerry said, 'For some reason, Peter thinks your car isn't working too well. He'll be calling to arrange to bring you to the party.'

'Oh . . . thanks.'

It worked like a charm. Jo and Peter arrived at the party together, and looking completely at ease in one another's company. Perhaps that did not augur well for romance, but it surely was a great basis for marriage, Kerry thought wistfully.

Everybody they had invited came. They lunched, al fresco, on the huge patio at the side of the house near the pool, and then sat in the shade, talking, relaxing, until eventually someone mentioned swimming. Peter was on his feet at once, shedding a gaily patterened shirt. He glanced round, caught Kerry's eye, and grinned.

'Race you, Kerry.'

'You're on!' Always happy to be in the water, she slipped out of her cover-up, revealing a slim turquoise maillot. She looked at Peter. 'Four lengths?'

'Right!'

Each watching the other, lest they steal a start, they moved to the edge of the pool, then, with one accord, dived in cleanly, barely disturbing the surface of the blue water. Kerry swam as though water were her natural element. Peter had the advantage of strength and muscle, but Kerry was quicker on the turns, and when they turned for the last lap she was half a length ahead. He overtook her gradually as they raced down the pool, but her hand touched the end a fraction of a second before his. Breathless and laughing, they clung to the edge of the pool.

The guests had all joined in the fun, cheering on first one, then the other, and now were applauding loudly. Above the noise, Alicia's high, penetrating voice was heard. 'Quite a performance!'

The laughter drained out of Kerry, leaving her deflated and selfconscious. Did Simon too think she had made an exhibition of herself? She glanced at him. He was looking down at her, and there was reassurance in his eyes. Next minute he was on his feet, saying, 'Let's all cool off.' Soon the water was full of people, splashing and laughing. Jo had not joined the others in the pool but was sitting on a long lounger, watching. Kerry lifted herself from the water, found her towel and dropped to the floor beside Jo. They sat in comfortable silence for a few moments, till Kerry heard Jo say softly, 'Do look at that.'

Following the direction of Jo's eyes, Kerry saw Alicia

delicately descending the steps into the pool. She must have been disrobing in the change room behind them. Jo, sotto voce, continued, 'Can that be cellulite I see before me? Would you believe? The perfect Alicia has big thighs!'

Kerry added, in the same low tone, 'And just a shade too much on the hips too.'

'And really, not *quite* enough on the bosom Yet, her figure has always looked so perfect. Do you think—falsies?'

'Perhaps a padded bra.'

They giggled together, like two schoolgirls.

After a moment Kerry said, 'I feel much better after that appalling display of felinity. I even think I can forgive Alicia, now that we know her dreadful secret. To think what those jodhpurs have been hiding, all these years!'

'And what's more,' said Jo, 'I don't think she can swim.' Alicia was playfully splashing water at Simon and squealing affectedly.

'No wonder she tried to put you down. She must have been green with envy, seeing you swim like that.'

'Believe me, I didn't mean it to be a spectacle.'

'Everyone knows that, including Alicia.'

Jo sobered, then said, a little selfconsciously, 'By the way, thanks for the advice about my car.'

'That's OK. Any time.'

'Was it so obvious?'

'That you cared about Peter? No. I only picked it up at the Hospital Ball because my own antennae were more sensitive than usual.'

'Simon?'

'Yes. That's when I really knew I loved him.'

'And now you're married to Simon, and Peter hardly knows I exist.'

'Give him time,' advised Kerry.

'I don't know whether I should tell you to butt out, or keep up the good work.'

'I'll be discreet if I feel a matchmaking urge coming on. I can tell you now, Jo, until the Ball I thought it was Simon you were carrying a torch for.'

Jo looked surprised, but considered the thought. 'In a way, I was, and am. But not like that. I worship him from afar—I always have—but I would never have aspired to marry him.'

'But Peter?' Kerry asked encouragingly.

'Peter is perfect, of course, and . . . more human.'

'Peter's a darling—a very warm, lovable darling. I think you were made for each other, and I wish you all the luck in the world.'

The guests lingered. Aunt Thea kept up a never-failing supply of goodies to nibble, and Simon filled and refilled long glasses with cold drinks.

He was a charming host, conversing affably with everyone, affectionately aware of his young wife, for everyone to see, with a hand on her shoulder here, a smile of encouragement there, an arm round her waist as they stood, saying goodbye to parting guests.

'A lovely party.'

'Thanks so much.'

'Like old times.'

Jo and Peter stayed for a last drink. Aunt Thea rejected Kerry and Jo's offer to help clear away, and they all flopped into deep, comfortable, chintz-covered armchairs, in the huge family room, reviewing the afternoon, agreeing that yes, it had been a marvellous party.

Peter eyed the pool table and said to Kerry, 'If I had the energy, I'd challenge you to a game.'

Simon said, 'If you're hoping to reinstate your masculine superiority, you might be sorry. My wife is a surprisingly versatile young lady.'

That night, encouraged by the success of her party and the increased empathy between them, Kerry asked Simon, as they stood outside the door of his bedroom on their way to bed, whether she might come in and talk a while.

He seemed a little taken aback, running a hand through his hair, but said, 'Yes, of course.'

He pointed her to the only chair in the room, a bedroom chair covered in deep cerise velvet. He sat down on the end of the queen-size bed, stretched his legs straight out in front of him with his hands clasped between them, and asked, 'Well, were you happy with your party?'

'Yes. Everybody seemed to enjoy themselves.'

'You realise we'll get a spate of return invitations now.'

'I suppose so.'

The longer this very ordinary conversation went on, the harder Kerry would find it to say what she had determined to say, so she took the plunge.

'We've been married for almost six weeks now, Simon.'

'So?' He was clearly on the defensive.

'It's been very different from what I expected it would be—in fact, very different, I imagine, from most marriages. I don't know whether you intended it to be like this when you married me, or whether something has happened that's made you regret doing so. I haven't come to beg for my 'conjugal rights', as they say, but I do think I deserve an explanation of why I don't seem to have any.'

There! She had said it, and she had managed to keep her voice and her manner calm as she said it. But she felt anything but calm as she waited for Simon's reply.

He looked a little pale but his voice, too, was controlled

as he said, 'I've realised that we were going to have to talk. I should have come to you, but I just haven't known what to say to you—I still don't. I'm deeply sorry about how things have turned out with our marriage, but I can offer you no explanation that wouldn't make the situation worse, except to say that no, I didn't intend it to be like this, and that you haven't been to blame in any way at all. I had no idea it would all be so difficult. If you want to leave me, I shall do everything I can to make it easy for you.'

This was infinitely worse than anything Kerry had anticipated as a result of their talking. She said in a small, strangled voice, 'Is that what you want?'

'No. But I can't promise you that things will be any different if you stay.'

'Will you tell me this one thing—is it Lori?'

His gaze fastened on her with something of the intensity it had that first day in the service station. He stood up, walked to the window and looked at it as though he could see out through the drawn blinds into the darkness. She could not see his face as he said, 'Yes. It's Lori,' but he sounded like a man tormented.

Without thinking of anything but his need, she stood up and went to him, clasping his arm with both her hands and laying her face against the rough tweed of his coat sleeve.

'Then won't you let me help you? I love you, Simon, so much! Please . . .'

For a moment she thought he was going to fling her aside, battling to control himself. He looked down at her and said, 'I know you do. That's what makes it so damnably unbearable.'

'Why should it?'

She lifted her face to look at him and did not try to hide the love and compassion she felt for him.

Simon closed his eyes and turned his head away.

'Then would you be prepared to stay a little longer, under the same conditions, and see whether . . . things . . . change?'

'Yes.' Kerry's pride seemed to have deserted her, swallowed up in her love for him.

He swung around as if amazed at her response. Then she was in his arms and her body was clamouring for his. Just let her break through his physical resistance now, she prayed, and his emotional problems, whatever they were, could be solved.

For a moment his arms held her closer and she thought she had won, but he let her go so suddenly she almost fell.

She regained her equilibrium and walked to the door. She knew she could not take any more. At the door, she stopped and said, 'I shall stay for three months. I won't raise the subject again or make any further approach to you in that time. Goodnight.'

CHAPTER TWELVE

KERRY lay awake for hours, going over and over her conversation with Simon, trying to make sense of it all, forcing herself to face the fact that her marriage was likely to drag on at its present low for a few more months, then peter out—'in shallows and in miseries', she thought.

She did not have to wait for that to happen. If she had any pride she would leave at once. But she knew she would not. As long as there was the faintest hope that this problem—whatever it was—could be resolved, she would stay.

There were other things to take into account too. There was her work. She had accepted the challenge to make the Unit function efficiently, and she wanted to achieve that. Then there was public reaction to consider. That would not affect her as much as it would Simon, as she would probably have left Mount Myall before the news of their separation broke. But Simon would have to stay and live with it. It would cause furore enough if she left after six months. After six weeks? It was unthinkable!

Her digital clock was showing four-fifteeen before she dropped into a heavy sleep. When the alarm woke her two hours later she was tempted to phone the hospital and say she was sick, so exhausted did she feel.

For the first time, she was several minutes late reporting on duty. Her senior nurse, McCusker, took one look at her and asked, 'Are you all right, Sister?'

Kerry knew that her looks would have belied her had she said, 'I'm fine, thanks.' So she had to admit, 'I'm not feeling very well this morning, Nurse.' Then she added,

'But it's nothing to worry about.'

Nurse McCusker had noticed for some time that Sister had moments when she seemed peaky and listless. She had had her suspicions as to the reason for this, and now she felt her suspicions were confirmed. She was discreet enough to mention them only to her closest friend, in confidence, but word quietly passed through the hospital that Sister Martyn was pregnant.

Such a possibility was so far from Kerry's mind and she was so preoccupied with her work and her problems at home that she completely missed the import of the occasional meaningful enquiry after her health, or of certain small acts of consideration that came her way in the following weeks.

She and Simon settled into what Kerry thought of as a holding pattern. They behaved towards one another very much as they had when Kerry had stayed in the house while Aunt Thea was away, for Aunt Thea and Davey's benefit, they greeted and farewelled one another with a kiss. Neither Davey or Aunt Thea was qualified to assess that there was a certain lack of the ardour between them which one expected of a newly married couple.

Kerry arrived home on the day following her conversation with Simon to find that he had gone riding. 'With Alicia,' said Aunt Thea, disapprovingly.

Why did he always turn to Alicia when he was upset? And how much did Alicia know about their marital problems?

He returned home from riding in time to spend half an hour with Davey before Davey's bedtime. That night, Davey had a bad attack of asthma.

A week later Kerry went to Simon's study one evening. He was sitting behind his big desk, with medical journals spread around him. He seemed reluctant to take his attention from them and jotted one or two notes before putting down his pen and looking at her questioningly. Kerry came straight to the point.

'I've discovered the cause of Davey's asthma.'

'You've *what*?'

'I believe I know what triggers his attacks,' she repeated.

'We all know what triggers his attacks. I do! Or do you have some theory that all the specialists and therapists have missed?'

Kerry ignored the sarcasm and persevered.

'It's quite simple, really. It was right under our noses and yet we missed it—perhaps because it *was* so simple. Simon,' she said quietly, 'has Davey ever been tested for an allergy to horses?'

'No. But he never comes in contact with horses.'

'But he comes in contact with you, when you've been riding.'

'You mean . . .?' Simon was watching her intently.

'I mean that every attack of asthma he's had since I've known him has followed contact with you, after you've been riding.'

He was frowning, exploring the implications of her statement, half convinced, with hope dawning in his eyes.

'You're sure of this?'

'I made sure. A few days ago, after he'd quite recovered from his last attack, I took your riding jacket—I'm sorry, I had to go into your room to get it.' Simon waved that aside impatiently.

'Davey had no idea what I was doing. I sat beside him, brushing the coat—to clean it, I told him—while he was doing his homework. Within five minutes he was wheezing. I had no doubt after that.'

'If you're right . . . it does seem to fit . . . Neither Lori nor I rode before . . .' He shook his head, bemused. 'Neither of us rode. And David didn't have asthma until I came back after Lori's death. That's why they believed I was to blame. And I was, too, if you're correct, but not in the way we all thought.

'I'll order a skin test immediately—tomorrow. I hardly dare hope. But if you're right, he can be desensitised. Kerry, I can't say how much this would mean to me.'

'I'm delighted for Davey too.' And for you, she thought, because you'll be freed from the load of guilt you've been carrying for two years.

The skin test proved positive and the desensitising process was begun.

They settled down again to a sort of friendly co-existence, but Kerry was never unaware of the passing of the weeks. She had no idea what Simon was thinking or how he was feeling. He seemed relaxed and even suggested they might give another party. This time they decided on a barbecue and tennis picnic. A barbecue would free Aunt Thea of much of the work of preparation, but she and Kerry filled the freezer with pavlovas well in advance and, on the day, prepared great bowls of salads. The tennis party was as successful as the pool party had been, and nobody, watching Kerry and Simon together, could have guessed that all was not well between them.

Simon's attitude towards Davey was much more relaxed and natural than it had been, and Davey blossomed, seeming to grow taller within a matter of a few weeks.

One morning, Simon left early for the hospital, saying he had a long theatre list. Aunt Thea departed too, to drop Davey at school and then go to a bridge morning and luncheon at the home of one of her friends. Kerry was not on duty till two o'clock, having changed her times to accommodate the Sister who normally worked the afternoon shift. She planned a long, leisurely morning, doing small chores, writing a letter or two, reading magazines.

At nine-thirty the phone rang. It was Simon.

'Kerry—I forgot to mention that Alicia will be dropping in this morning to collect a book she lent me some time ago. It's a manual on horse riding and it's in the second drawer on the right of my desk in the study.'

'I'll find it.'

'Thanks. And Kerry . . .' He paused.

'Yes?'

'Have a good day.'

He hung up, and she was left wondering what he had been about to say. There had been a softness in his voice, a timbre that she could not interpret. She stood clasping the receiver lovingly, as if to hold on to the moment.

Then she remembered the reason for his call. Alicia was coming. Kerry could have wished her elsewhere this morning, but she would make sure her visit was as brief as possible, by having the book ready to hand to her when she came to the door.

She went along the hall to Simon's study. She had never been here alone before, and she stood for a moment in the doorway, savouring the aura of the room. It was so masculine, so distinctively his. The morning sun was casting a long finger of light across the deep blue of the carpet. She moved into the room, touching, caressingly, as she passed it, the leather of his armchair, where it bulged from his sitting in it. His desk was tidy, the few things on it neatly arranged—a writing compendium, a large pad, the telephone, an ebony desk set with two gold pens. Had that been a gift from Lori?

The second drawer, he had said. But had he said left or right? Kerry opened the second drawer on the left. It was almost full. On top were several medical journals, and she lifted these to look beneath them for the book, not quite knowing what she was looking for—a manual, Simon had said. Beneath the journals was a picture frame, lying face down. Curious, she lifted it and turned it over.

For a moment she was puzzled, hardly knowing what she was seeing. There was no way that Simon could have got a photograph of herself. She realised, almost immediately, that the face looking back at her from the photo was not really hers. There were subtle differences, but the likeness was amazing. The same fair hair, brushed off the face and waving gently to the wearer's shoulders. The same mouth, the same bone structure of the face, the same slender neck and lift of the head, so that grey eyes laughed up at whoever had been taking the picture.

She knew, before she saw the inscription low down against the frame on the right-hand corner, whose face she was looking at. 'To Simon, with love. Lori.'

Realisation came slowly, because her mind was fighting against accepting the truth that hammered at it.

She was still standing there when the door behind her make a small noise and she whirled around, expecting, illogically, to see Simon. But it was Alicia who stood there.

'I knocked, but nobody answered,' said Alicia. She took a step or two further into the room. Her eyes, curious at first, travelled from Kerry's white, stricken face to the photograph in her hand. Comprehension, sly and satisfied, dawned on Alicia's face.

'You said you knew why Simon married you. Whatever reason he gave you, you seem to have found the true one.'

Kerry said nothing. She was barely aware of Alicia's presence, only that her words were confirming what the photograph had already told her.

'So now you know! Simon was marrying a ghost when he married you,' the mocking voice went on. Then, as Kerry still said nothing, it became harsh, vindictive.

'You little fool! Did you think *you* could ever take Lori's place? And Simon's a fool too. I told him so at the picnic, when I first guessed what he was going to do. I know him so well, you see, almost better than he knows himself—certainly better than you ever could. And he threatened me—he actually threatened me—with what he'd do if I ever said anything to you about your resemblance to

Lori. Well, you've found out for yourself, and I haven't had to say anything, have I? I wish you both joy of what's left of your marriage.'

Afterwards, Kerry remembered Alicia's words as though they had been burned into her brain. But now they hardly seemed to penetrate her numbed mind. All she knew was that she must get rid of this hostile presence, so she could think what she must do. Alicia. Alicia had come for a book. The second drawer on the right, Simon had said. She went to it, opened it, mechanically, took out the book, which was lying immediately inside, and handed it to Alicia, saying in a small, controlled voice, 'Will you please go now?'

Alicia took the book and, after another long, speclative look at Kerry's pale face and burning eyes, turned and walked out.

Kerry, left alone, with meticulous care laid the photograph face down on the corner of Simon's desk. She had no further need of it. Her legs were suddenly weak, and she sat stiff-backed on the edge of the second armchair. Alicia's words were drumming in her mind, over and over. 'He married a ghost. He married a ghost.' It all fell into place, as though she had just found the vital piece of some puzzle that made sense of all the rest. Pieces that had never seemed to quite fit before now slipped smoothly into place. Things she had pushed to the back of her mind, because she could not understand them, or because she thought them unimportant, now rose up to mock her.

In some bizarre attempt to regain what he had loved and lost, Simon had married a ghost. Because she looked uncannily like Lori, he had thought he could recreate the life he had had with her before tragedy took her from him. Kerry had been the unsuspecting pawn in his attempt to do this. There had been nothing in it for her—he had never suggested that there was, had never told her he loved her. He had wanted a replacement—a replacement wife for himself and a replacement mother for Davey.

She made herself go back and begin at the beginning. No wonder Simon had looked as thought he had seen a ghost that day at the service station! It was the kind of thing that happens—a face in a crowd, that seems familiar, that brings the past tumbling back. He must have gone on his way, shaken, but not expecting to see her again.

And next day she had turned up in his hospital, on the staff and there to stay. That explained his hostility then. Then Davey, little, innocent Davey who could barely remember his mother, had taken to her instantly because she looked like Lori, and Simon had seen how he could turn it to his and Davey's advantage. Suddenly Jo's words came back to her—'There's nothing Simon wouldn't do for Davey.'

The thoughts and questions went round and round in Kerry's mind. Had he been coldly calculating about it all? Or had he gone into it, hardly knowing what he was doing or why, but driven by some wild hope about how it would work out?

No wonder he had often seemed withdrawn—haunted, almost. Now she could understand the contradications in his attitude towards her. The kindness, the occasional tenderness, the passion in the pool that morning—they had all been Lori's. The coldness, the remoteness, the sudden rejections, had been Kerry's.

She felt used, humiliated, denigrated.

No wonder she had seen a different Simon Travis from the one everybody else knew. Jo had said . . . Jo! Jo had known all along! Jo, who had been her friend, had allowed her to marry Simon, knowing that he was doing it only because she looked like Lori! Almost, she felt more betrayed by Jo, who must have, in cold blood, calculated the chances of it working out, than by Simon who was driven by heaven knew what devils of memory and desire.

Matron, too, had known. Kerry recalled her startled

look the first time she saw her. And how she had been unhappy at the idea of her marrying Simon. Why had she not told her the reason for her reservations?

The guests at the wedding! Many of them would have known Lori, would have seen the resemblance, would have known why Simon was marrying her. She felt physically sick at the realisation.

And Peter? She could not believe that Peter had known. He was too transparent to have hidden it. Perhaps he had not known Lori long enough or well enough to see the likeness. But, even had he done so, Kerry knew without doubt, he would have sacrificed her happiness in a minute if he thought it would help his 'Boss'.

She tossed the knowledge that Alicia had known aside. Alicia did not matter. It was the betrayal of her friends that devastated her. Well, their conspiracy had not worked out for Simon's benefit. She hoped they were all satisfied.

She felt utterly alone. There was no one in Mount Myall to whom she could go for friendship and sympathy. Aunt Thea? Yes, Aunt Thea had loved her for herself, and Kerry found the thought extraordinarily comforting, until she realised that Aunt Thea too, if it had come to the crunch, would have put her beloved Simon's happiness first, as had all her other friends.

She could never face them again. Most of all, she could never face Simon again. Her cheeks burned at the thought of the first night of their honeymoon. She had been so ecstatically happy, and he had simply been acting out his fantasies, in the consummation of their marriage. Then why had he rejected her later? Had he been stricken by compunction? Or had she not been . . . good enough, enough like Lori?

She had no idea how long she had been sitting there in Simon's study, but suddenly she was consumed by the need to get away before anyone called or came. Who knew but that Alicia might have rung Simon, to taunt him, as she had taunted Kerry.

The photograph of Lori still lay on the table as Kerry left the study and went to her room.

She took down the old suitcase she had brought from Sydney, not the smart one Simon had bought for their honeymoon. She selected and packed only those clothes she had had with her when she came. She did not stop to change the jeans and T-shirt she was wearing. The day was warm, but she felt cold and shivering. She had some money in her purse and her bankcard would get her to where she was going.

She walked out of the house without a backward look and leaving no note. Let Simon explain to everyone why she had gone. She would not give notice at the hospital, would never contact them again. She owed none of them anything. They had all betrayed her, used her, hurt her, as though *her* feelings and *her* happiness had simply not mattered, only Simon's.

Her Maxi was in the driveway, and she tossed her case in the back and got behind the wheel. She chose a back road out of town in case anyone saw her.

The road wound in and out amongst rolling hills and farm properties. Its surface was loose and gravelly. Kerry was driving fast, to put distance between herself and Mount Myall.

As she swung around a bend she saw a cow standing in the middle of the road and slammed her foot on the brake. The cow turned its head, mildly interested, as the car skidded out of control and crashed, with a sickening crunch, into a large tree beside the road.

CHAPTER THIRTEEN

'SISTER! Sister Martyn! Are you awake?'

The voice was persistent, reaching down, dragging her up from oblivion. Someone was patting her cheek, not very gently then raising her heavy eyelids. The light bothered her and she resisted, turning her head aside and frowning because it hurt to move her head.

'You're awake, Sister—that's good! Everything's fine! Just go back to sleep.'

Silly of them, waking her up to tell her to go back to sleep. But the voice was reassuring even though she could not figure out why she needed to be reassured. A beep-beep beside her she knew was a cardiac monitor. She had a leaden feeling in her side and her head felt abominably fuzzy as well as hurting if she moved it. She was too sleepy to put all these facts together and work out where she was and why. Someone else could do the thinking for her. She felt quite peaceful, really. She went back to sleep.

When she woke again the beep-beep was still there. It was a familiar sound and its rhythm was steady and strong. No problem there. She knew now that she was in the Intensive Care Unit. She could see a Sister, through the glass, talking to Dr Travis. They raised their heads as the beep-beep changed rhythm momentarily. In an instant they were standing beside her.

Now there was something else—a dark cloud hovering. Kerry didn't want to think about it. She closed her eyes and turned her head as cool, firm fingers felt for her pulse. Stupid—Dr Travis didn't need to feel her pulse with the beep-beep telling him she was just fine.

'How do you feel, Kerry?'

His voice was kind, professional. Without opening her eyes she nodded, then realised again that her head defintely should not be moved.

She did not want to talk to Dr Travis. As long as she didn't have to talk to him she need not think about that dark cloud. Thinking was like her breathing now—it didn't hurt as long as she didn't do it too deeply.

The drugs they gave her kept her sleepy and she had little awareness of the passing of time. Efficient hands sponged her, turned her, settled her into her pillows. Pain throbbed in her side and there were other places that were stiff and sore. More kind hands gave her an injection. There were voices—all concerned and kind—Jo's, Matron's. More often than not, when she awoke Dr Travis was there.

On the third day they moved her and the tubing and paraphernalis to which she was attached from Intensive Care to a private room with special nurses for day and night. Her medication was reduced and she slept less.

Gradually, though she fought against it, memory returned and she could no longer keep the dark cloud at bay. She was too weak to stop the tears that came and kept coming, so they had to give her more sedation. Post-anaesthetic depression, they said it was.

Simon came, late that morning. By then an artifical, drug-induced calm had followed the weeping, though her eyes were still red-rimmed and dark. She was not at all sure she could maintain the fragile calm in his presence.

He asked, 'How are you feeling?'

Now that she was fully conscious, his voice was hard and there was a stiff rigidity in his face and an ocean of reserve in his voice, as though he were the one who had been wronged. He was upset that she had been trying to run away. But surely he did not blame her?

She did not reply to his question, not trusting herself to speak. Anyway, he knew, better than she did, how she was.

He said, 'I had hoped we would have been able to talk today. But you're still very weak and I think we'd better leave it until tomorrow. But not longer than that.'

Kerry nodded miserably. 'Yes, the sooner the better.'

He left, and she had a day and a night, between waking and sleeping, to think about what they would say to one another.

When he came the next morning, he gestured for the nurse to leave them alone and stationed himself at the foot of her bed, looking down at her, propped on pillows, her hair loose about her shoulders, her eyes very wide. She was glad the sedation she had had earlier was still effective.

Simon's hands held the rail at the foot of the bed and she saw him loosen his grip as though forcing himself to relax.

'I know you're not well enough for a long conversation but, in your own interest, I have to ask you one question.'

'Yes?'

'Are you pregnant?'

Stupefied, she could only repeat the question.

'Am I *pregnant*?'

'That's what I asked. I need to know for medical reasons.'

Kenny found her voice with difficulty and said in choked tones, 'You, of all people, must know the answer to that.'

Some of the tension seemed to drain from her face.

'Then, if you're not pregnant, there's no more to be said.'

'Oh, yes, there is!' Her anger overcame her weakness. 'There's plenty more to be said. I demand an explanation of why you asked me such a question.'

Simon looked round for a chair, as if finding it suddenly imperative to sit down. He seemed to be searching for words, as though the conversation had taken a turn he had not expected.

'I'll explain. Before I began operating on you, someone in the theatre said, "But what about her pregnancy?" I said you were not pregnant and everybody seemed to accept that. But I kept wondering, as I operated, whether it might be true and, if so, how the surgery would affect your pregnancy. Since then, I've been careful to order drugs that would be less likely to harm a foetus. I could have ordered a pregnancy test without your knowledge, but that seemed underhand. So I've had to wait until you were well enough to be asked.'

If Kerry had not had sedation she knew that she could not have controlled her emotion as she listened to his monologue. When he had finished she said, in tones as deliberate and measured as his had been, 'Since if I were pregnant by you the pregnancy would have been in its fourth month and would have been evident when I was on the table, I can only assume that you suspect I might have been—sleeping around?'

Simon looked at her with misery in his eyes, clearly wanting this traumatic conversation over and done with.

'Not sleeping around, exactly. I did wonder about . . .'

'About whom?'

'Peter.'

'Peter Treloar?' The situation was becoming farcical, soap-operish.

'You must admit you were very friendly with him before we were married. And you made sure he was invited to your parties.'

'*Our* parties. Peter and I are good friends, but I'm not in the habit of going to bed with people just because I'm good friends with them.'

He looked as though he would have suggested that they not finish the conversation, but Kerry had not had her say, by a long way.

She sat forward, off her pillows, disregarding the pain in her side and facing him angrily.

'From the time we first met Simon Travis, you've put the worst possible construction on everything I've done. You've judged me and condemned me, without bothering to find out what sort of person I am. In the past I've had many friends, several romances, plenty of opportunities. But because I have old-fashioned ideas about love and marriage I reached the mature age of twenty-three years and managed to remain a virgin. Apart from two lapses—which I now bitterly regret—I would still be so.'

She lay back, exhausted, and closed her eyes. She never wanted to see him again. Then she realised that there was something else which might as well be said now. She opened her eyes, to see him looking alarmed and his hand reaching for the bell. She stopped him with a gesture.

'While we're on the subject of relationships, I could reciprocate by asking you about Alicia—not that it will make any difference to anything, but it might be interesting to know just how double your standards are.'

Simon's voice was drained of all colour as he said, 'I know my name has been linked with Alicia's. But since Lori, and apart from those . . . lapses . . . you mentioned, I've never been able to bring myself to be intimate with another woman.'

'Then I suggest you get over that hang-up before you ask somebody to marry you, next time!'

He turned, without a word, and left the room.

Kerry felt weak, drained and conscious of a great loss. Where there had been hopes, dreams and expectations, there was nothing but anger, disappointment and hurt.

That afternoon Meg Thornton, Sister in charge of the ward Kerry was in, brought in an exquisite arrangement of flowers—deep red roses, white carnations and light-as-air gypsophila. She held it so Kerry could read the card attached. 'Kerry, with love. Simon', then began rearranging other bowls of flowers to give pride of place to this very special one.

Kerry said, 'Don't bother, Meg. Put them there,' indicating an empty spot on a table where they would not catch her eye and remind her of her misery. They were Simon's gesture of apology for his suspicions of her, but it would take more than that to heal this final wound.

Meg was still fussing with the flowers and persisted till she had found a prominent spot to display them. So not only could Kerry see them every time she raised her eyes, but everyone who came into the room could read the card, with its message of love.

Perhaps it was better, Kerry thought, to keep up the pretence that all was well between them. Simon must have done so, since the staff clearly had not the slightest inkling that there was anything amiss. It would be much easier for her to likewise perpetuate the myth.

Now that Kerry was feeling a little better, several visitors were allowed in briefly. Bitterness welled up in her heart when Jo, beaming brightly, popped her head round the door and asked permission to come in. Kerry found she could not respond to Jo's friendliness, and Jo, concerned for her, did not stay long.

Aunt Thea came, tearful and anxious, and Kerry clung to her for a moment, as much to reassure Aunt Thea as to take comfort from the kindly old soul's concern for her.

At seven o'clock, Simon came again. Nothing more was said about the conversation of that morning. They talked of trivialities, like two strangers.

'How are you feeling?'

'Better, thank you.'

'I'm glad.'

'Thank you for the flowers. They're lovely.'

'I'm glad you like them.'

It was not long before he said, 'You're tired. I won't stay.' He touched her hand, momentarily, and was gone, but his brief visit had set the pattern for their behaviour in the future.

Kerry intended that future to be as short-lived as possible. Just as soon as she was physically able, she would leave Mount Myall, telling no one in advance. And this time she would not bungle her departure.

Until now, she had not been interested enough to find out the full extent of her injuries. The staff had not been specific, assuming, probably, that Dr Travis would have told his wife all he wanted her to know. Now she needed to know, for her future plans.

When he called next day she asked him. He looked surprised that she did not know.

'I had to do a splenectomy. I thought they would have told you that.'

'I suspected it because of the site of the pain and the sutures. Was that all?'

That was the major thing. Apart from losing your spleen you've lost a fair bit of blood and a couple of days that you won't ever remember much about. You had multiple minor injuries and mild concussion and you'll feel stiff and sore for a while yet, but we want to get you up and moving as soon as we can. Perhaps tomorrow you can start mobilising.'

There was something Kerry had not mentioned before but thought she should do so now.

'I'm sorry you had to do the surgery,' she said.

Simon's mouth quirked. 'I hope you don't have reason to be. I think I did a good job.'

'I meant—I'm sorry you had to operate on your—wife—for the second time.'

'Oh, that!' He carelessly brushed it aside. 'Not to worry—this time was different.'

Kerry bit her lip. He still had the power to hurt her. Did he have to be so cruel? She forced herself to continue the conversation.

'How did the cow get on?

'What cow?'

'The cow on the road. I can't remember whether I hit him . . . her or not.'

'There was a cow on the road?' He seemed pleased to know there had been a cow. 'I wondered what made you hit the tree. We thought you'd been speeding and gone out of control. Or . . .' He bit off what he had been going to say, and added, 'The cow must have got off scot-free. Certainly it had left the scene of the accident by the time you were found.'

'And how's the Maxi?'

'The Maxi is a write-off, I'm afraid.'

'Poor Maxi.'

Not having the car would complicate her departure next time. But she would manage, somehow.

Even though they had talked about the accident, Simon had made no mention of the suitcase in the car. Nobody else seemed to know about it. Aunt Thea could not have refrained from mentioning it, had she known. Kerry wondered how he had managed to keep it a secret from her, and how long it would be before they talked about that too.

Jo's next visit was a longer one. Kerry tried to appear normal towards her. For one thing, she had questions she wanted to ask Jo.

'Jo, why did *Simon* have to operate on me? Surely there must have been someone else?'

'There was, but Simon insisted on doing it. He didn't hear about the accident until after you'd been brought in and he was absolutely frantic.'

Kerry had her own ideas about that, but she said

nothing.

Jo went on, 'If he hadn't got himself in hand by the time you were prepped and ready for surgery, they wouldn't have let him go ahead. But it seemed so vitally important to him that he do it that the other surgeons just had to give in. Dr Cornwall assisted and Dr Samuels stood by, ready to take over if Simon didn't seem up to it. But he was never better. Drama! I tell you, Kerry! You should have been there.'

Kerry held her side as she joined in Jo's laughter. This was a different version of her operation and one that interested her greatly. She prodded Jo to tell her more.

'Who gave the anaesthetic?'

'Peter. Who else?'

Then there had been more drama in theatre than even Jo realised. Peter—the anaesthetist—as Simon operated on his wife, suspecting that she was pregnant by Peter. Phew!

As if prompted by Kerry's train of thought, Jo said, 'And of course, to add to the drama, there was that story that had got around the hospital that you were pregnant. When someone mentioned it, Simon just said, "No, she's not," and that was that. But we were all thinking that husbands aren't always the first to know these things and what if you were and hadn't told him. What effect would the surgery have? Simon must have been thinking the same. But he was wonderful. Imagine being loved like that!'

Jo heaved a long sigh.

Kerry said brightly, 'Your turn will come.' But she was thinking, Frantic with anger, frantic with jealousy. But never frantic with love.

Jo said, 'We were all so thrilled when we heard you might be pregnant, Kerry.' She looked at Kerry hopefully, but Kerry shook her head.

'Sorry. Not this time. And not . . .'

Her eyes brimmed with tears and Jo was contrite.

'I'm sorry, kid. I've stayed too long. Now don't you worry about it. If you're not pregnant this time you will be soon enough. It's early days yet.'

Kerry's tears flowed the more and Jo patted her arm, trying to comfort her. Kerry made an effort and said tearfully, 'I guess you've heard all about my post-operative depression. At first they called it post-anaesthetic depression—now it's post-operative—I wonder where we go from there? It's so embarrassing. I never know when I'm going to drown everyone with floods of tears. They've all been so marvellous to me and all I can do is weep at them. Would you believe, I very rarely cried before I came to Mount Myall.'

Perhaps she should not had said that, but Jo accepted it without question.

'I guess you miss your folks too, just now, you poor kid. Anyway, don't worry about the tears. I'm sure everyone understands. After all, they're nurses too, and they know about depression as a drug side-effect. Now that you don't need so many pain-killers you'll soon be over it.'

But Jo's prediction did not come true, and nobody could do anything about Kerry's tears because nobody knew the reason for them. They suggested anti-depressants, but she refused and tried to fight it alone, but it went on and on.

They kept her in hospital long past the time when she would normally have been discharged. She did not mind that, because the longer she stayed the less time she would have to spend at home with Simon before she was strong enough to leave.

Simon accepted that she stay in hospital. Perhaps he had suggested it because he too dreaded their being in the house together.

The days were uneventful. Kerry pushed herself to walk a little further each day, so she would become stronger quickly. She was dressing now and wandering round the hospital, even going as far as the Nurses' Home, where she spent time chatting with off-duty staff.

Matron had made a daily visit from the beginning, but Kerry could not feel the same respect and admiration towards her as she had before. Jo came daily, and Kerry found her bitterness towards Jo lessening. After all, she had done what she had out of love for Simon and hoping that it would work out for the best for both of them.

Kerry noticed that Peter's name was cropping up frequently in Jo's conversation, and one day Jo bounced into the room, saying, a little selfconsciously, 'I've brought someone to see you.'

She beckoned and Peter's red head popped around the door. He had been to see Kerry several times, but this was clearly a special occasion.

He and Jo stood hand in hand at the foot of the bed, beaming, and Kerry beamed on them.

'Need I ask what this means?'

'No, just give us your blessing.' This was from Peter, with a grin that split his face.

'Bless you, my children. I don't need to say how happy I am for you. Now tell me—how, when, where?'

'Look at her! All wide-eyed innocence! As though she hasn't plotted and schemed and . . .'

'All right! But when?'

Peter replied, 'Looking back, I realise now that it began, for me, anyway, at your wedding. It's usual for the best man to kiss the bridesmaid—or so they told me. And of course, we were really inspired by the way the bride and groom kissed. But it took a sledgehammer to get it into my thick skull, and your not very subtle scheming to get us to your pool party together was the clincher.'

'I really am so thrilled. I've dreamed about this happening. And your beloved Porsche—how is it fitting into the scheme of things?'

'It's a fitting conveyance for my queen of hearts,' with an affectionate look at the blushing Jo.

More than two weeks had passed since the accident before word went round the hospital that Kerry was being discharged. On her last morning she received a steady stream of visitors—doctors, nurses Sisters, orderlies, who came to wish her well and say they had never had a better patient. They all said they hoped to see her back at work soon, but not too soon, to take it easy and get really well again. Kerry knew that it was a final goodbye that she was saying, over and over that morning, but she was careful to avoid any such suggestion as she said, " 'Bye for now," "See you soon," "Thanks so much for everything." '

As she walked carefully down the steps to Simon's car, his arm was protectively round her waist, and none of the little group who watched and waved from the top of the steps could have suspected that all was not well between them.

At home, Aunt Thea received her with a breathless spate of welcoming words, interspersed with tut-tuts about her being so thin and threats to fatten her up now she was home again. Davey was at school. Simon joined them in the sunny living room for morning tea and then left for the hospital, saying, with what appeared to be genuine concern, 'Take good care of her, Aunt Thea.'

It was a quite unnecessary admonition. Aunt Thea was determined to do just that and, on the first day, Kerry submitted, allowing herself to be put to bed and waited on. She had to admit she did not feel as strong as she had thought herself.

Davey came home. He was thrilled to see her, but Kerry was pleased to see, already, a new independence and confidence in him. He was full of his involvement with Cub Scouts, and looking forward eagerly to a camp that was planned for the May holidays. Kerry was reassured that he would be better able to handle her going than she had dared hope. At the same time, it occurred to her that then might be the ideal time towards which to plan her own departure.

The next morning set a pattern for the weeks that followed. Aunt Thea insisted that Kerry remain in bed till mid-morning and brought her breakfast on a tray. Simon dropped in, spent a few minutes with her, then dropped a kiss on her brow before leaving for work. It seemed that it was not going to be the difficult period Kerry had feared.

She was up and dressed in time for a walk around the neighbouring streets before lunch and would spend the afternoon reading, relaxing, occasionally watching a daytime soap opera on television—something for which she had rarely had time before.

Either Simon was very busy or was finding excuses to be out of the house a great deal. When they did meet in the context of family life, he was courteous, as he would have been to a guest in his home.

As they all sat at table one evening after dinner was finished, Kerry said, 'I've been wondering whether I'd be wise to take a holiday while I'm convalescent. Matron said I was to have all the time I needed, and I would very much like to see my family.'

Aunt Thea said, 'That's a good idea. You still look very peaky.' Then she looked at Simon, as though fearing she had been presumptuous to speak before he had a chance to.

Simon turned on Kerry a long, considering look. If he suspected what she had in mind, he did not say so, merely agreeing, 'It would do you good. Matron tells me that changes you made in Casualty before your accident are working out well. She's eager to have you back to complete the transformation, but she wouldn't expect you to return until you're completely well. Where would you go, and when?' he asked.

'Sydney, for a start, to my brother and his wife. Then I would want to spend some time with my father in Cairns.'

'They've all been very concerned about you,' said Simon. 'Your father must have spent a fortune on phone calls while you were in hospital.'

'I've been missing him . . .' Kerry could feel those treacherous tears welling again and she suppressed them angrily. She must not allow herself to become maudlin with self-pity. She hoped the others had not noticed.

'Davey has a Scout camp in the May holidays. I thought I could go about the same time,' she said.

'I could drive you to Canberra and you could take a flight from there,' Simon said.

'Oh, no!' she protested. 'It's not worth the bother. The bus is quick and comfortable, and air-conditioned too.'

'You're sure you'll be well enough by then?'

'I'm improving every day, and that would still leave me a fortnight to prepare.'

There would be no hitches this time. After she had been away a few weeks she would write to say that she was staying on longer. Finally, she would write, briefly, giving no explanation, simply saying that she would not be coming back. Simon could make any explanation he wished. By then, Davey would have adjusted to the idea of life without her. Aunt Thea would have her two men to look after, and now that Davey was so much better that would be much less worrisome for her. And Simon? It was no concern of hers what Simon did when he was free.

Matron, Jo, Peter, the hospital staff—some might suspect what had happened, but unless Simon told them they would never know for sure. It would be a nine days' wonder, but it would pass. Kerry told herself that the only thing she regretted leaving was her job in Casualty. She hoped Matron would find someone to take over where she had left off.

Kerry came back from her own thoughts to hear Aunt Thea speaking, tentatively as usual.

'I wasn't going to mention it—I wasn't thinking about it, really, with Kerry sick and everything. But there's a bridge convention in May in Hamilton. If Kerry is going to be away and Davey is at Cub Scout camp, might it be possible—just for a few days—I'd leave everything prepared . . .' She looked at Simon anxiously, expectantly.

'That's a great idea. You must go, Aunt Thea. You've had a lot of extra work and worry with Kerry's illness and you deserve a break. I shall manage very well on my own for that short time.'

It was all working out. This time there should be no hitch, thought Kerry.

During her first week home, she had had very few visitors from the hospital, she thought. But in the second week, as word got around that she was going on holiday to Sydney, she had a steady stream of callers, all of them warm, friendly, wishing her well. She tried not to think how happy she could have been at Mount Myall if things had worked out differently.

The hardest parting was from Jo. The last of Kerry's resentment towards Jo evaporated when she came to say goodbye.

After a lively session of hospital gossip and shop talk, Jo got up to leave. They walked together to the front door. Jo looked at Kerry and suddenly there were tears in her brown eyes. She tried to hide them by giving Kerry a quick hug and saying huskily, 'You get better and hurry back, kid. We're going to miss you. I'm really sorry about what we've all done to you.'

Kerry was not sure whether Jo was merely referring to the accident, or whether she had guessed that the marriage had not worked out and was feeling guilty that she had not warned Kerry against it.

Kerry returned the hug and said, 'Thanks, Jo, for everything—your friendship, for being you—just everything! And look after Peter.'

Jo was her old buoyant self again. 'That reminds me—Peter and I are starting to make plans, and they include you. So write to me as soon as you know when you'll be back. Imagine, two staff weddings in one year! The hospital hasn't had so much excitement in ages.'

With another cheerful, 'Goodbye,' Jo moved off to her car. She opened the door and turned to wave, but by then she was too far away to see that there were tears in Kerry's eyes now.

Davey and Aunt Thea, both simmering with excitement, left on Wednesday afternoon. Kerry was to leave the following morning.

Kerry held Davey tightly for a moment, then dropped a kiss on his head and released him before he had time to protest. He had become very scornful lately about what he called 'kids' stuff'. Going to his first camp overshadowed everything else and he was barely aware that Kerry was going 'on holiday' too.

Aunt Thea kissed Kerry goodbye rather distractedly, amid a spate of last-minute instructions to Simon about where he would find this, what he should eat first of the provisions she had prepared for him, where he could contact her if need arose.

Then Simon and Kerry were alone in the house, which felt, suddenly, very empty and strange. The evening and the night stretched before them. Aunt Thea had left a meal prepared. They ate in almost complete silence, then carried their dishes through to the kitchen and put them in the dishwasher. Kerry excused herself, saying she still had some packing to do and wanted an early night. Simon seemed hardly to hear her, so she repeated her 'Goodnight' and went to her room.

She had been given several sleeping tablets when she left the hospital, and she felt that this was a night when it might be wise to take one. She slept soundly and wakened only to the clamour of her alarm next morning.

She ate breakfast on her own in the kitchen. Later her path crossed with Simon's once or twice as they moved about the house. They exchanged a remark or two, but that was all.

By ten o'clock she was ready to leave. The bus was not due to pass through Mount Myall until ten-thirty, but she wanted to be at the station in good time in case it gained a little time, as it sometimes did. There must be no slip-ups this time.

She said a silent goodbye to the house. Simon carried her suitcase to the car, then came back to lock the door behind them before assisting her into the front passenger seat. It was unseasonably warm—a real Indian summer—and promised to be even hotter later in the day. Kerry was wearing a yellow frock and white sandals. Her legs were bare.

The short drive to the bus station was uncomfortable and she fervently hoped that the bus would not be running late. She dreaded the moment of farewell with Simon, and the sooner it was over the better.

She remained in the car when they arrived, while Simon went to the back of the car to get her suitcase from the boot and book it through at the office. He seemed to be a long time behind the car, and she heard no sound of him unlocking the boot.

She was surprised, yet in a strange, fatalistic way, not so, when he came back, opened the door on the driver's side and got into the car, closing the door behind him.

His face was very pale and taut as he said, 'Kerry, am I correct in thinking you don't intend to come back?'

She could only nod, numbly.

'I shan't try to make you change your mind, but I can't let you go without saying certain things first. Would you come back to the house for a short while? I promise you I shall make other arrangements for you to leave, later today.'

She turned her head away from him, looking unseeingly through the window. For a few moments she battled with herself. Then that same feeling of fatalistic resignation resolved her conflict and she knew she would do this last thing he asked of her.

She looked at him. Almost imperceptibly, she nodded her head.

CHAPTER FOURTEEN

IT WAS cool and dim in the house, after the sunshine and heat outside, and very quiet. Neither spoke as Simon led the way to the sitting room. Kerry was glad he did not take her to the study. She had not been there since the day she had found Lori's photograph, and she was still feeling too emotionally fragile to face a flood of memories of that day.

As she entered the sitting room, Simon halted by the telephone in the hall. She heard him dial a number and then, almost immediately, speak briskly. 'Greta? Would you make a reservation on the late afternoon flight from Canberra to Sydney, please. I'll ring you later for details.'

He walked into the sitting room and across to where Kerry was sitting.

'Are you comfortable?' His hand reached towards a cushion, but she nodded her head, saying, 'I'm quite all right, thanks.'

'Would you like a cup of coffee?'

It was not like him to fuss, as he was doing now. She guessed he was putting off the moment of saying whatever it was he had brought her back to say. Perhaps he needed time to know how to say it. If she was not to catch a plane until late afternoon, they had plenty of time, so she said, 'Thanks, that would be nice. But tea, please.'

Simon went to the kitchen and she could hear the clattering of cups and tea-pot and of water running as he filled the electric jug. She looked around the room of this house she had loved from the beginning. Always, even in the bad times, it had ministered peace to her, and now, having returned to it again after what she had thought was her final farewell this morning, she could sense its almost tangible welcome. She would still be leaving, but, for the short time that her departure had been deferred, she would be in this house she loved, with the man she had loved. She felt incredibly calm and at peace.

Simon returned with the tea-tray and placed a small table at her right hand. He poured milk into a cup, then added tea and brought it to her. She smiled up at him, with a quiet, 'Thank you.' A flicker, as of sudden pain, crossed his face and he looked away. But by the time he had poured himself a cup of tea and sat down opposite her, he seemed calm, although his face was still pale. He began, in level, controlled tones.

'Thank you for coming back, Kerry. What I have to say won't take long. I'm arranging a flight for you to Sydney, from Canberra, and I'll drive you to Canberra in time to catch it. But I couldn't let you go without putting the record straight. There's been too much misunderstanding from the very beginning of our relationship. Before you go, I want you to know just what my position has been, and is. Perhaps then you'll be able to forgive me, or at least, not think too harshly of me when you take up your new life, wherever that may be. Please hear me out, without saying anything?'

He looked at her questioningly. She nodded.

'When you had your accident you were running away because you'd found Lori's photograph and realised how much you resembled her.'

It was a statement, not a question, and Kerry made no response.

Simon went on, 'I saw the resemblance to Lori the first time I saw you—I couldn't have missed it. It was uncanny and it quite unnerved me, reviving, as it did, all sorts of memories. But I didn't then, in my wildest dreams, expect to see you again. So it threw me completely when I met you the next day—in the hospital, in uniform, and obviously there to stay.

'I think I hated you then—you were so much like Lori, and yet you weren't Lori—just a ghost come back to haunt me, a ghost who was a complete stranger—you knew nothing of what you were doing to me and you could give me back nothing that I'd lost.

'Subconsciously, I suppose, I thought that if I made things unpleasant enough for you, you'd leave. I'm not proud of that, but try to understand. It had taken me so long to get over Lori's death and, just when I thought I was succeeding, you appeared and opened up all the old wounds.'

Kerry protested, 'Is this really necessary? It's very painful for both of us.'

'Please bear with me—it won't take long.'

She shrugged and subsided. The best thing for both of them would have been for him to say nothing, just let her go. Eventually, the wounds would have healed.

But he seemed to have opted for radical surgery, and if it would help him to go through it step by agonising step—if he could find some sort of absolution in the telling, then she would listen. She was prepared to do that one last thing for him because, as much as he had hurt her, as much as she had refused to acknowledge the fact in the time since the accident, she still loved him. She almost despised herself for it, but she could do nothing about it.

Simon had known that she loved him. She had made no secret of her love. She flushed to think how ardently she had gone to him . . . when all the time . . .

At least he would never know that her love had survived the trauma of the last weeks. He would assume that it had died on the day when she had found Lori's photograph and had known why he had married her. He had used her and deceived her, but at least he had stopped short of the ultimate deception of saying he loved her.

She made herself listen to what he was saying now.

'David, of course, took to you immediately because you reminded him of his mother. But it wasn't only that. You also gave him the warmth and affection and acceptance he needed—and that I seemed unable to give him. I think my feelings of guilt and the knowledge that I was responsible for his asthma blinded me to his real needs.

'I suppose it was partly for David's sake that I asked you to marry me. But it was jealousy of Peter Treloar that made me propose as soon as I did. He was so young and handsome and full of fun, with his life before him, not living in the shadow of a tragic past, as I was. I believe you, now, that there was nothing between you and him, but the way things were going there could have been, and I had to do something before that happened. And then having you in the house and feeling so much that you belonged here. I genuinely had become very fond of you—in a fatherly sort of way, I thought.'

He paused, remembering, despondent.

'I think I'd begun to come to my senses before the wedding. I should have stopped it all then before it was too late. But you seemed so happy—I was pleased that you were and I couldn't bring myself to spoil it. And I kept telling myself that it would all work out in the end . . . It was our wedding night that brought me to my senses—made me realise what I'd done and face the reason why I'd done it. It was your love and your trust . . .'

His face contorted. His hands were tightly clenched.

'Can we leave it there?' Kerry's voice was thin because her throat had tightened unbearably.

Simon seemed not to hear but went on. 'I've never felt such an utter, despicable heel. I couldn't go on pretending—living with you as husband and wife. But neither could I bring myself to tell you why I couldn't. I had no idea where it would end, but just kept hoping that some day in the future it might resolve itself.

'In the midst of the whole sorry, confused state I was in, there was one thing I hadn't realised. It was everything that happened on the day of your accident that brought me to my senses—hearing that you were badly injured, realising that you'd been running away from me, thinking you might be pregnant by Peter, having to operate on you knowing that you could slip away from me as Lori had done—it hit me like a thunderbolt from the sky. I loved you—yourself—Lori had nothing more to do with anything as far as we were concerned.'

A small, strangled sound escaped Kerry's lips, but he held up a hand for silence. She sat, with eyes downcast so that he could not read what was in them, drinking in every delicious, unbelievable word, wondering how long she could contain the happiness that was welling up in her.

Simon still talking, as though the one important thing now was to finish his story, to get it over with.

'And then, no sooner had I realised that I loved you than I had to face the fact that you despised me, and I couldn't blame you. The way I'd deceived you, rejected you as a wife, accused you of infidelity with Peter, knowing that you couldn't wait to get away from me for good . . . I've made my own hell and I'm going to have to live in it for a long time. But I couldn't let you go without knowing the truth—I want no more deception. And, however hopeless it is, I had to tell you that I love you.'

He still did not look at her, as if he did not want to make any appeal to her emotions, merely to make known the facts. He stood up, like a man who has been in a dream awakening to reality. 'I'll go and ring Greta to get the details of your flight.'

'Simon!'

He swung around at the sound of Kerry's voice, tender, pleading. He looked at her and she did not have to say anything more.

'Is it possible?'

'It always has been—even in the bad times.'

'My darling!'

His arms were open and she went into them, to be clasped and held. And this time she knew that there would be no rejection, no cruel thrusting away. She raised her face to his. His eyes were full of wonder as he looked at her. Then his mouth was on hers in a kiss she thought would never end. She did not want it to. Because this was heaven. And heaven is for ever.

'Kerry,' Simon said at last, and there was urgency in his voice. 'You are my wife . . .?'

'I want to be . . . so much!'

With an exclamation of joyful disbelief, as though he could not yet grasp what was happening, he folded her to him again, in a long, gentle caress. Then, very tenderly, he lifted her and carried her into his room.

Kerry had a fleeting moment of wondering how she would explain to everyone why she was not, after all, going on holiday. All she knew was that her next holiday would be a honeymoon.

Then even that ceased to matter.